Nell

Annie Seaton

Pentecost Island

Book 3

Dedication

To best friends all over the world. There is nothing like female friendship.

Acknowledgements

A huge thank you to my editors and proof-readers: Susanne Bellamy, Roby Aiken and Kristen Woolgar.

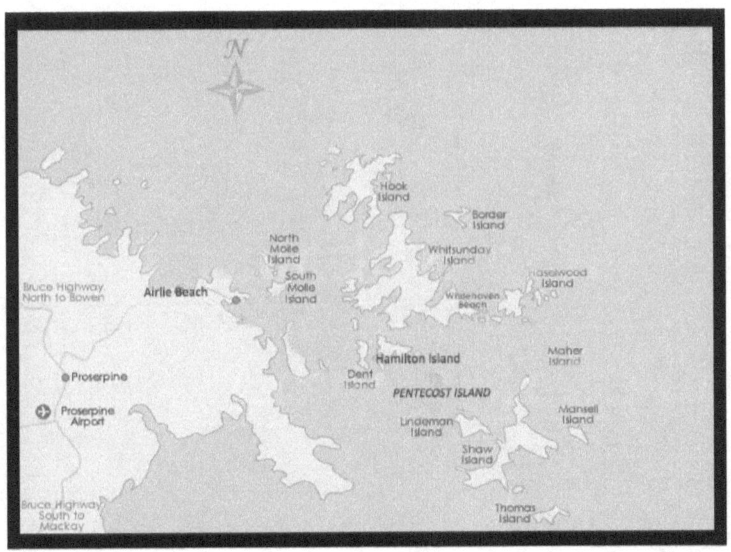

WHITSUNDAY ISLANDS

Chapter One

University of Queensland, Brisbane…2010

Nell O'Leary was bored stiff.

And cranky.

She stretched out her legs and pointed her toes, and then rolled her ankles. Fiddled with her bracelet, flexed her fingers and tapped her pen on the desktop in front of her seat. Leaned back, rolled her shoulders and tried not to yawn. Looked down and admired the pretty ballet flats she'd chosen to match her dress. Hummed a song in her head and then blushed when Nat Dwyer, the student she always sat with, nudged her.

Oops, maybe it hadn't been in her head.

There was a lot of pen tapping, doodling, and staring into space by most of the students around them as Professor McMinn went on about macro and microeconomics.

The monotonous voice of the most boring lecturer in the university, Professor McMinn, droned through the speakers. It was an additional lecture that had been added to their timetable just for this week. The same night that *Cat empire*, her favourite band, was playing in the university bar. Tonight's lecture was scheduled to go until nine o'clock and knowing old, dry and dusty McMinn, it was sure to go over time. Tam and Pippa had promised to save her a seat in the bar, but she'd be lucky to find them in the crowd she knew would be there. They'd be dancing now, and, where was she? Trapped in boredom city.

The lecture was a compulsory one—with nonattendance threatened as due cause to fail the course—and each student had to sign in when they entered the massive lecture hall. Nell looked around and smiled before she leaned over to nudge Nat.

'Easy to see why we had to sign in. I don't think anyone would have come tonight if it hadn't been compulsory,' she whispered.

'Yeah, he's a crafty old bastard.' Nat leaned over as he replied quietly. 'Not to mention as bloody boring as bat shit.'

Nell stifled a giggle. Nat was always able to make her laugh. They'd met up at the beginning of first year and were good mates. 'And we're only halfway through.'

'Have you decided on your major for next year?' he asked, keeping his voice low. His minty breath brushed her cheek and she gestured to the pack of mints on the desk and smiled as he handed the packet over.

'I'm changing courses,' he said as she popped a mint into her mouth.

Nell nodded and whispered back. 'Yep, me too. I'm going to switch across to accountancy. This economic stuff bores me to tears. What about you?'

'I'm moving across to a computer degree. It's what I want to do. My old man told me economics was a better choice. He was way wrong.'

'Better choice for you, that's for sure. You've saved me a few times over the past two years.'

'That's only because you don't back up your work, and then you can't find where you save your files.'

Nat's chuckle was low. 'You have to get better organised, Nellie girl.'

Even though they were in the second back row, Professor McMinn had eagle eyes and was glaring at them as he spoke.

'Ssh. We've been spotted.' Nat elbowed her and stopped talking.

They both sat up straight and pretended to be focused on the ins and outs of microeconomics.

One very long hour later, the professor nodded and turned off the microphone.

'Thank God, for that,' Nell said as she stretched her arms above her head and rolled her neck before she stood.

'That's two hours of our lives we'll never get back,' Nat gathered up his books and pens and mints and then stood beside her. She looked up at him as he towered over her; he was a great-looking guy. His blond curls—always tangled—were well past his collar now, and his brown eyes were fringed by thick dark lashes.

'Coming to the Student Union to hear the band?' she asked. Nell was happy with the relationship she had with Nat. They had different friends but occasionally ended up at the same parties. He was smart and funny, and she knew she could trust him, but no matter how gorgeous he was, she'd never considered going out with him.

Not that he'd asked her.

Maybe because he had such a reputation as a lady-killer. As much as Nell liked to dress up and party, he was out of her league.

"Love 'em and leave 'em" was Nat's attitude. Or so it seemed to Nell.

Friends was good, and friends they'd stay.

She stared at him and wondered idly if he'd ever thought about asking her out. His gaze stayed on hers and for the first time ever, her tummy gave a funny little flip and her fingers tingled.

'What's wrong?' he asked with a frown.

She shook her head quickly. 'Nothing. I was waiting to hear if you were coming to hear the band.'

'Nope.' His white teeth flashed in his tanned face. 'I've got a hot date.'

'You've always got a hot date. Selina?' Nell asked. At least she thought that was the name of his most recent lady.

'Nope,' he said as they walked out. 'A hot date with a fileserver over in the medical faculty. My mate's the computer tech over there and they can't get it to back up to tape every night.'

'Boring.' Nell rolled her eyes. 'Why don't you come over to the bar when you're done?'

His eyes held hers for a little longer than they usually did. 'You know what, Nellie. I might just take you up on that.'

'See you there, maybe.'

'Yeah, baby, yeah,' he responded in his best Austen Powers voice.

'Oh, behave,' she came back at him with a cheeky grin.

Nat winked and took off towards the door.

Chapter Two

Pippa: 2020

'Don't stress, Nell. We'll get it sorted.' I gently placed my hands on Nell's shoulders as she sat in front of the computer in the space at the front of the house we'd turned into an office and reception area. Her shoulders were rigid, and I could feel the tension radiating through her body. 'It's not that important in the scheme of things.'

Tam and Evie had gone to bed, and I'd been heading over to Rafe's when I'd come across Nell in the office, her shoulders shaking and her face in her hands. Eliza and Phillipe had flown out of Hamo airport today, headed for the UK. I'd left it later than I usually did to go across to Rafe because he'd been waiting for a video call from Jenny and Bryant, his publishers.

'It is important!' Her tone was full of worry and I frowned as it was so out of character. Nell was usually cool and calm—the one who always told *us* to chill, and it upset me to see her stressed.

'This is going to impact on the whole business. Everyone has worked so hard. Ma Carmichael's resort is *your* baby, and your leadership has been so motivating, not to mention the great advertising campaign you've created. Tam's got the kitchen running like clockwork and the new menus look fantastic. Evie has the gardens looking a picture, and Eliza worked her butt off to get the huts finished before they left, and I've let you—'

'Nell.' I crouched down in front of her and tried to make light of the situation. 'And you've just been sitting at your computer playing computer games, while we've all worked hard, have you? Give yourself a break, chickie. You might be in the office, but I reckon you've put in more hours than the rest of us. I've seen the light on in here in the middle of the night when I've come out for a drink. You're not kidding anyone.'

'Only when I can't sleep,' she mumbled.

'Now let's look at this logically. Tell me exactly what the problem is, and we'll come up with a solution.' I stood and crossed to the chair beside hers and sat down. 'Two heads are better than one.'

Finally, a glimmer of a smile. 'Thanks, love, but it's not that easy. I've talked to a few of my contacts down in the city, and some online forums, and I'm sure it's a networking problem. I'm an accountant, and I can sort out all the software stuff, but my skills don't stretch to networking.'

'You can't get anyone to log in remotely for you?'

'No, it's a physical issue, I think.' Nell shook her head. 'But the bottom line is, I've lost all the bookings we had for the first month, and all of the accounting stuff has disappeared. *And* Tam's food orders to the mainland supplier.'

'But you've backed it up, you said?'

'I did,' she said glumly. 'But I can't find that either. I think you're going to have to find someone who knows what they're doing a bit more than I do.'

I reached across and took her hands in mine. Despite the warm night, Nell's hands were icy. At school, she'd been the chubby one of us but she'd lost weight when we were at uni, and never put it back on. I think she thought the shorts and loose tees she wore hid how thin she was, but she hadn't fooled Tam and me.

'Don't you ever dare think that. I wouldn't care if we had a scrap of paper to write the bookings on and an old-fashioned ledger book for the accounts. We're all in this together, girl.'

Nell chuckled and her eyes brightened a bit. 'Well, *I'd* care.'

'Let's make a plan then. We've got four weeks until our first guests are in the huts, and a week before the bar officially opens for business full-time.'

We'd had a few casual afternoons in the bar when boats had moored off the island, and their crew had come into the beach in their tenders. The word about the bar—that Rafe had christened Gilligan's—was spreading. It had been good for Tam too, the informal start; her bar food had gone down very well. We'd decided to have an unofficial opening for those regulars who were starting to call in every few days

Eliza had been pleased they were still here for the opening before they left. Our casual sailors had all come back and the bay was full of boats. Phillipe had put channel markers along each side of the channel and fifteen boats had been tied to palm trees along the sand. Business was so good we'd all taken turns to help Tam behind the bar.

'Gotta get more help, Pippa,' she'd said as she flopped into a chair at the end of the night. 'I can't keep this up.'

Eliza and Philippe could have stayed another two weeks for the main opening, but understandably she was super keen to get back to see her family. Plus, she had a lot of financial sorting out ahead of her with her deceased husband's estate apparently in chaos.

'I need a favour, Pip.' Nell leaned back on her chair and rubbed her eyes when I went into the office later that night. 'One of my contacts in Brisbane told me that the computer store in Proserpine has a networking guru on staff. I'll get you to take me across to Hamo tomorrow and then I'll catch the ferry across to the mainland and hire a car. I need to talk to someone face to face, not online or over the phone.'

'Okay, on one condition,' I said.

'What?'

'As long as the cost of the ferry and the hire car and any other costs come out of the business. You might have to stay overnight if you miss the last ferry back.'

She looked at me over the top of her glasses and then nodded reluctantly. 'All right. But I have a condition too.'

'Hmm?' I raised my eyebrows at her.

'If we lose any bookings or any money because of my stuff up, I'll put some of my savings into the business, and I won't take any pay until it's all sorted out.'

'No.'

She leaned back and folded her arms. 'Then I guess we're at a stalemate.'

'No.'

She stared at me and didn't look happy.

'Nell? It's not your stuff up. You've worked so hard, putting yourself in here night after night. You don't have fun like the rest of us. Yeah, we all work hard, but you've got to learn to chill a bit.'

'Are you saying that's why I'm making mistakes?' Her chin lifted.

'No, that's not what I meant at all. When Aunty Vi left me the island I came up with the idea of the resort and you and Tam came on board, and yes, my vision was to make a living, and make a profit, but also to have a great lifestyle here. Can you remember what you said in the bar at Surfers when I asked you what your dream job was?'

'If I could do any job we wanted, anywhere in the world, what would I choose?'

'That's the one.' I watched her expression close down even more and my worry increased. Tam, and Evie, and now Eliza, had taken to island life like I had imagined. And wanted them to. And as for me, I'd never been happier, but Rafe had a lot to do with that. But Nell? She always seemed so serious and unhappy. She was even quieter since we moved to the island at the end of autumn and lately she seemed to be spending less time with us when we went for a chat on the beach at sunset.

She worked too hard, long hours, and it was almost impossible to coax her out to the beach or the bar at night.

It was hard to reconcile this Nell with the girl Tam and I had gone to school with. When I thought about it, back in those days and in our early uni days, Nell had been the loud one, and the party animal at uni. She'd worn the shortest figure-hugging dresses and she'd always looked vital and attractive. She'd been the first to suggest a party, or going to the bar to see a band, or just hanging out with friends. As she'd got further into her studies, Nell had taken it so seriously her social life and her outgoing personality had been consumed by study and work.

'And what did you tell me your dream job was?'

'I said'—she tapped an ink-stained finger on her lip— 'somewhere warm. No winter, lots of blue skies, and near the ocean. And being in charge of a business. I think that's what I said.'

'That's it. And that's what you're doing. What we're all doing. Nell? Can I ask you something and get an honest answer?'

Her eyes were wary, but I got a nod.

'Are you happy here? Is it too quiet? Or claustrophobic being on the island? Or is the responsibility too much for you?' I hated asking that because I had no doubt in Nell's ability.

Her face reddened, and I noticed that she wasn't wearing her usual lipstick. Tam and I had often wondered when Nell had changed her style of dress and stopped wearing makeup, why she had only kept the red lipstick.

'No, Pip.' Her voice was fierce. 'I love living on Pentecost Island, and I love what I'm doing. I couldn't imagine going back to live in the city. We have a perfect life here.'

'So why are you unhappy?'

Her brows lifted in surprise 'I'm not unhappy. What makes you think that?'

I stared at her for a while. 'You don't seem to enjoy the sorts of things we do to chill. Or enjoy being with us all. Is it because it's not just the three of us now? Is it because we have Rafe, and Evie and Eliza and Phillipe? You seem to prefer being in here by yourself.'

Nell took a deep breath. 'I do prefer to be by myself. That's just me.'

I was shocked when her eyes filled with tears. I opened my arms and I was pleased when she accepted my hug.

Her voice shook. 'I love this job with you and Tam, and the others. I know it's a dream come true for you, Pip, but it is for me too. I can do what I love and not have to deal with people all day long. Setting up the network and the systems let me be in my own company. So of course, I want to stay.'

She wriggled away from me and I stepped back holding Nell's gaze steadily. 'I don't know what happened to make you feel that way, but I know something happened at uni. You changed almost overnight.'

'I learned to be responsible.' She kept her eyes on mine but there was a tinge of bitterness in her voice. 'It's just me. Like it or leave it.' I was surprised at her sass as Nell was usually quiet.

'Okay,'—I held up a finger and wagged it at her—'enough of this "more than you can handle" crap. Do what it takes to get it sorted, and you're not paying for one cent of it, or going without your pay, girlfriend. You got that?'

'All right.' Nell lifted a shaky hand and wiped the back of her hand over her eyes. 'You're the boss.'

'Only when I need to be. The rest of the time, we're equals in Ma Carmichael's.'

We walked out of the office and Nell looked up at the big clock in the hall. 'You're late going to Rafe's place. You'd better get going or he'll be over here looking for you.'

'He will.' I put my hand on Nell's shoulder and was surprised when she tensed. 'Now you get to bed and forget about numbers and computers for one night. I'll meet you down at the jetty at seven, and we'll go to Hamo so you can get the first ferry across to the mainland.'

I was thoughtful as I made my way up the hill to Rafe's house. I was going to have a chat to Tam. We needed to get to the bottom of what was wrong with Nell.

For her sake and the sake of our venture.

Chapter Three

Nell: Hydeaway Bay-50 kilometres north of Airlie Beach

The sun shone from a cloudless sky as Nell boarded the ferry the next morning. The passage was calm, and the mid-morning service was almost empty. The trip across to Port of Airlie was fast and Nell picked up a hire car in town and was on her way towards the computer store in Proserpine by lunchtime.

'Sorry, love. We only sell computers and fix minor issues here.'

'I called yesterday. I was told you had a networking specialist here.' Nell looked around the store as if to conjure up a technician.

'Well, you weren't talking to me. Probably that useless bloody apprentice I've got.' He shook his head. 'Do you know how hard it is to get a kid who wants to work and learn these days? I thought I'd hit the jackpot with the new bloke, but he changed his mind. Said it was too far from the islands, moved further north, Bloody hell, it's only half an hour.' He settled back, ready for a chat—and a whinge by the look of things. 'More competition for me.'

Nell tried not to snap back; the day started off well and was fast going downhill. 'Can you tell me where to find him please?

'Up to Hydeaway Bay. Do you know where that is?'

'No.'

'Go up the highway a bit and take the Gregory River turn off and head for Dingo Beach. It's about fifty ks north.'

'Do you have an address please?'

He scrawled on a scrap of paper and handed it over.

'Thank you.'

Before she left the small town, Nell decided to do the shopping there that Pippa and Tam had requested. There was a good kitchen store there, and by the time she had found all of the obscure things on Tam's list and picked up some art supplies for Pippa's advertising, her stomach was growling with hunger. She sat in a small bakery, and had some lunch, enjoying being away from her computer and desk for the first time in many days.

An hour later, she regretted taking the break. Five different lots of road work on the short stretch of highway, and then a wide load moving a huge piece of mining machinery up the highway added almost two hours to her trip.

By the time Nell approached Hydeaway Bay the sky had clouded over and the weather was closing in. Pippa had been right; she was going to have to find somewhere to stay after she talked to the networking guy. She sent a quick text, so Pippa knew there was no need to take the boat back to Hamo to pick her up this afternoon.

The forecast had been for a late storm, and for once, the weather bureau had been spot on. Nell leaned forward, her attention focused on the road ahead, as the clouds grew darker and the wind whipped the low-hanging branches of the trees into a frenzy. She clutched the steering wheel of the unfamiliar car tightly as the dirt road petered to a track. She hated storms and wind, especially at night. Some nights when they had first arrived on the island, Tam and Pippa had sat out on the veranda watching the wild weather come in across the passage.

Nell had hated storms since her days at Queensland University. She shook her head and swallowed.

Don't go there.

She peered through the windscreen as she put the wipers on to the fastest speed. The rain was getting heavier and it was hard to see where she was going.

Surely this couldn't be the right road?

The address the guy had scrawled said *ND IT Services* 655 Dingo Beach Road, Hydeaway Bay, and when she'd pulled over and checked her phone, the signpost about five kilometres back had confirmed that she had taken the correct turn. The sat-nav system had her going in the right direction. It was the right road—although it was more a track—and Nell was determined to find the blasted place.

Frustration vied with anger, and she considered turning around, but the track was so narrow it would take a ten-point turn to go back the way she'd come.

Besides she *had* to see this guy.

As she'd left the computer store owner had assured her that he was very good and would go out to Pentecost Island to solve her problem. In fact, he told her that the guy was so good, several businesses on Hamilton used his services, so he should be able to come out to Pentecost Island without a problem. Maybe she should have gone back to the island, and just called him.

Nell shook her head as she peered ahead. No, this had to be sorted quickly, and she could convey that urgency much better with a personal visit instead of by phone or email.

But it was heading for five o'clock and now she was worried the store would be closed when she got there. She'd tried to call, but the phone had gone to voicemail. She'd left a message and a quick outline of the problem, so at least they knew she was on her way.

Finally, a gate appeared ahead and in the fading light, she could just read the number 655.

'Thank God,' she muttered under her breath. This was her last chance; if this guy couldn't help her, the opening of the resort was at risk. It was too late to get someone to fly up from the city and look at the problem; the bar opening was less than a week away, and she just couldn't let Pippa down.

She *wouldn't* let Pippa and the team down.

The gate was closed, and Nell pulled over to the side of the road. The track was so narrow, another car couldn't get past her anyway. She climbed out of the car. She put her hand over her eyes to stop the rain blurring her vision.

With another frown, she looked ahead as she hurried across and pushed the gate open, again doubting that she had the right place.

'I've come this far, I might as well keep going,' she muttered closing the gate behind her.

Sure enough, a timber sign on the small dwelling ahead read *ND IT Services*, and Nell puffed out a sigh of relief.

Finally.

But then she frowned. Despite the sign, this wasn't a store or an office, but a private house, and there were no other houses within sight.

Nell swallowed and wondered if she was game to continue. The wind whistled and the tree branches creaked against each other as it picked up more speed.

I have to. I will not let the girls down.

A light was shining in the front window and she set off across the front yard looking nervously at the long grass that brushed against the bare skin below where her shorts ended.

Please, no snakes.

A flash of lightning was followed immediately by a huge crack of thunder that shook the ground. She took off from the gate and ran through the long grass and up the two steps at the front of the house.

Nell came to a stop on the veranda and raised her hand to knock, but the door swung open before her knuckles could connect with the timber.

With a gasp of disbelief and dismay, she took a hurried step back. She teetered on the edge of the veranda, but a hand shot out to grab her arm before she could fall backwards down the steps. The last time Nell had felt this bone-chilling fear she'd been nineteen and halfway through her accountancy degree.

'Careful, sweetheart. I don't have any public liability insurance.'

Her heart thumped hard and her mouth dried as she stared into the eyes of the man she had once been close to. It might have been a long time ago, but she had never forgotten—or forgiven him.

Her voice was low and angry. 'What the bloody hell are you doing here?'

He narrowed his eyes and looked at her, and she knew the moment that recognition dawned.

'I could ask you the same thing, Nellie.' His voice was as deep and smooth as ever and Nell shook his hand from her arm as her skin crawled beneath his touch.

Chapter Four

Nell

'It's been a long time,' Nathaniel Dwyer said.

'I'm leaving.' Nell turned around to the stairs, but as she took the first step a bolt of lightning hit a large tree on the other side of the gate, followed by a deafening roar. Goose bumps rose as static ran up her arms and the smell of something burning surrounded them as she stared at the tree now cleaved right down the middle. Half of it had landed across the gate that she had walked through only minutes ago. It had missed the hire car by centimetres.

'Don't be silly.' Nat opened the door and gestured for her to go inside. 'I don't think you're going anywhere for a while.'

She stood there and stared at him, before turning and looking at the sky. Dark angry clouds pierced every few seconds by lightning forced her to make the decision she didn't want to. But she had no choice.

Reluctantly Nell looked at the open door and took a step inside.

'Wise choice.' He closed the door behind her and gestured for her to follow him. 'Come down to the kitchen.'

Nell took a deep breath as she followed Nat into the house. She squeezed her hands into fists and her nails cut into the skin of both palms.

He led her down a narrow hall towards the back of the house. On each side the doors were closed, and as they walked past, a loud humming noise was evident despite the rain that hammered on the tin roof. Finally, the hall opened out into a large kitchen and there was room to keep her distance.

A large old-fashioned kitchen.

The old wooden cupboards reminded her of the kitchen in her grandparents' house at Sandgate. When she was a child, they had visited there every Saturday and her Nana had made pink lamingtons, especially for Nell.

Those visits had been a treat. She would sit at the end of the old Laminex table eating cake and drinking lemonade while Dad played cards with her Nana and Poppa. In the background was the constant noise of the Saturday horseraces on the transistor radio punctuated by Dad's and Poppa's call of 'Mugs Away' every few minutes. They had kept the visit routine going after Mum had gone.

When Nell had finished her drink and cake, she had been allowed to go underneath the old Queenslander by herself and watch the chickens hatch in the specially heated incubator under the house. Poppa had had chickens for as long as she could remember and—

'Nellie?'

She blinked and lifted her gaze from the table that had brought those memories to the surface. Nat stood there scratching his head, with a quizzical expression on his face.

'It's Nell,' she said crossing her arms.

Nat looked at her, his brow wrinkled. 'How did you know I was here at Hydeaway Bay?' he asked. 'And more to the point what are you doing here?'

Nell took a step back and put her hands behind her back, clutching at the kitchen bench behind her. If she held it tight, she could control her shaking hands.

If she'd known that she would be in a house by herself with him—with any man, but even worse with Nat Dwyer—she would not have opened the gate. By now, she would have been roaring back down the road towards the ferry, the island and her safe haven. What had she been thinking to set off on this journey?

You were thinking of Pip, and the resort, a stern voice told her.

'I didn't know it was you.' Nell was quite proud of how firm she managed to keep her voice. 'I guess you must be the local networking expert I have heard about.'

'Was that you who left the message on the phone earlier?' he said slowly. 'From some new resort over on the islands?' As he gestured to a chair, he pulled out another one and sat down. 'Please. Sit down.'

She nodded but remained standing. 'Yes, that was me.'

'So how can I help you? I thought you were working down at the Gold Coast.'

He'd kept tabs on her. Nell tried to speak but her mouth opened, and nothing came out. Her heart thudded and her mouth was as dry as a bone. She jumped when Nat stood suddenly and pushed his chair back and crossed the kitchen towards her. He walked past her, and she tried not to cringe as he reached into a cupboard and took out a glass before filling it with water at the sink. He handed it to her and held her gaze steadily, but his voice was gentle.

'Are you scared of storms, Nell?'

She nodded and he gestured to the chair again. Let him think that, it was better than him knowing that she was terrified of being in the house with him.

'Sit down, and you can tell me why you need my services.'

Keeping one eye on the door, she pulled the chair out and slid into it.

'Are you hot? Would you like me to open the door?' His voice was quiet.

Nell watched as Nat flicked the lock over and opened the back door, pushing a chair against it so the wind didn't slam it shut. She let herself really look at him now that they were inside. Nat had lost weight over the years. When they'd been at uni, she'd teased him about the amount of time he'd spent working out. Those years of happy teasing were a long time ago. He'd conned her for a long time, and eventually showed what he was really like. The long tangled blond curls were gone, along with the board shorts and surfie look. She'd grown up fast, and it looked like Nat had grown up too.

Through the screen of trees in his back yard, she could see the dark sea surging onto a beach that was at the back of his house. The wind was roaring outside, but the noise of the waves crashing on the beach soothed her.

Because she knew she could get out that door if she needed to.

Nat walked around and sat in the chair opposite. 'Last time I saw you, I think you were working in the accountant's office where we set up a new fileserver. Broadbeach, wasn't it?' His tone was conversational and had lost the aggression that it had held when she had been at the front door. 'I guess you must be working up here now if you are looking for networking help. Are you still in the accounting game?

'I am, and yes I do need help.'

Thank God the words came out this time.

Even though they sounded breathless.

'I'll give you a brief rundown of what we need and then I'll be on my way.'

Nat shook his head and she tensed. 'You won't be going anywhere for at least a few hours. Probably not until the morning. This storm is going to get worse before it gets better. I've been up here a couple of years, and I've seen some doozies.' He looked up at the ceiling, and she followed where he was looking. There was a big circular water stain on the ceiling above the fan.

'I was here when Cyclone Debbie hit, but this old house is solid and there was no major damage.' Nat chuckled and it was like being back in the lecture theatre beside him. 'The only damage was to my mental health. I thought I was going to be stuck in this house listening to the wind for the rest of my life. Were you up here for the cyclone? Is that why you're scared of the storm?'

She shook her head and managed to speak again. 'No. We've only been up here for a few months.'

'We?' he said with raised eyebrows. 'Husband? Kids?'

'No. Pippa and Tam and me, and some others.'

'Wow, it must be ten years since I've seen them.' Nat's eyes widened. 'Not since we were at uni. What are you all doing up here? Working?'

'Pippa has a resort on an island and I'm looking after the office. Front and back end. We have a networking problem that needs immediate attention, or we are in trouble. You were recommended.' She took a breath and relaxed a little more.

'And the last person you'd want to help you would be me, wouldn't it? Looks like you're stuck between a rock and a hard place, Nellie, because I'm the only one who can help between Mackay and Townsville.'

The Nathaniel Dwyer of old was back.

There was no way she was going to spend the night in this house with him.

Chapter Five

Nat

Nat found it hard to stop looking at Nell. She was different to when they'd been at uni together. She'd lost a lot of weight, and by the look of things, she'd changed in more ways than that.

When they'd been mates in first and second year, she'd been full of life and sass. She'd met life head-on, and she'd had the best sense of humour; it was hard to believe that this fragile-looking woman was the same Nell he'd known.

After Nat changed degrees and took up computing science, he hadn't seen her around campus much, and he'd only seen her once since uni, and he'd regretted that meeting for a long time.

The night they'd had that boring lecture with McMinn—it had been so boring he could still recall it almost ten years later—Nat had looked into her eyes and felt an absolute jolt go through him. They'd shared an Austen Powers joke, and he'd had full intentions of going down to the bar after the computer job he had to do.

By the time he got there and went looking for Nell, she'd gone. Tam and Pippa were there, and Nat had asked where she was.

'Gone home,' they'd screamed together over the music as they'd danced. The gloss left the night, and he went home.

I'll see Nell in lectures or on campus, and ask her out, he'd thought.

That had been his plan, but it had never happened. He'd got busy—between his study, his computer jobs and the bar work he did to supplement his student allowance—there was no spare time to socialise. Nell for some reason, took to sitting in the back row of the lecture theatre by herself, and Nat took the hint. But it had hurt.

He knew he had a reputation for being a bit of a player on campus, but that had suited him. He didn't want to get tied down into any relationship. He had a career and a life ahead of him, and he was way too young to settle down.

Uni finished, and they all went their separate ways. Nat got called to a job three years after graduation, and there was Nell in the office where he was supposed to be fixing a fileserver.

He'd sauntered over to her desk and put his well-practised charm to what he had thought was good use.

'Nellie. What a great surprise!' Nat leaned on the corner of her desk and looked down at her.

Surprise filled him. Her usual smile was nowhere in sight, and the drab khaki T-shirt made her face look sallow. Her pretty hair was scraped back into a tight ponytail, and the only colour was a vivid slash of red lipstick, that somehow looked bizarre.

She looked up at him as though he had just crawled out from under a rock, but Nat ignored it, thinking she hadn't recognised him.

'Yeah, baby, yeah?' he ventured in his best Austen Powers accent. 'It's me, Nat.'

'I know perfectly well who you are.' She gestured coldly to the receptionist who was standing near the door. 'Charlotte, can you please show Mr Dwyer where the computer room is.'

She had turned her attention back to the computer and he had been dismissed. The whole time Nat spent in the back room fixing the fileserver, he stewed; her attitude had pissed him off. It made him wonder what he'd done to make Nell ignore him those last few months in lectures, but he knew he hadn't done anything to her. He'd been judged on his reputation, and that made him angry.

But to this day he regretted the way he had spoken to her on the way out. When Nat walked through the foyer, Nell was standing at the front desk talking to the receptionist. The drab T-shirt was tucked into a pair of knee-length black shorts. On her feet were joggers and white socks. What had happened to the pretty feminine Nell? But despite her appearance, that old jolt of attraction had rocked through him.

'And don't ever speak to a client like that again, please. It was unnecessary.' Even though her words were soft, he could hear the grilling that the poor receptionist was getting. It must have been the joke the girl had told him on the way in.

Nat shook his head as he walked past and caught the eye of the receptionist. She put her head down and he could see tears glinting in her pretty eyes.

'It's okay, love,' Nat said. 'Nervous Nellie here could take some lessons in manners from you.'

He wouldn't have said any more, but Nell followed him to the door and then outside the building. Her face was white—apart from the that slash of red lipstick—and she pointed at him as she spoke.

'I would appreciate you minding your business when you are in our workplace. I'll be contacting your employer and making a complaint about your attitude.'

Nat had shaken his head. 'Jesus, Nell. What's happened to you, the kind and pretty girl who used to joke with me back at uni?'

'It's all about that, isn't it?' she snarled. 'What we look like, and how attractive we might be to the male of the species.'

He took a step back with my hands up and put on his best Austen Powers voice. 'Whoa, baby. What's your point?'

Her stare was glacial, and she turned and opened the door.

'For God's sake, Nellie. I'm joking. Chill.'

'Grow up, Nat.'

The door closed in his face, and he couldn't help having the last say. 'Not so shagalicous these days, baby,' he'd called through the door.

It was a cruel barb, and Nat regretted it as soon as the words came out of his mouth, and he hoped she hadn't heard the insult. He'd thought about calling her and apologising afterwards, but she had turned into such a cold fish, he decided to let it go. She never did call his boss anyway.

Now as he looked at her sitting at his kitchen table, it was as though those years had not intervened. The same khaki shorts and T-shirt, and the same red lipstick. The same closed expression.

Nell stood and gripped the back of the chair. 'If that's the case, and there are no other local experts, I'll get someone to come up from Brisbane. I won't bother you any longer.'

Nat kept my voice calm. 'Let's go back to the beginning. Forget we know each other. You need some network help, and I can provide it. No past, no insults, no nothing. Okay?'

Her hands let go of the chair and she nodded slowly. 'Yes. I need someone to address the problem very quickly.'

'How about I make coffee and then you can tell me what the problem is.'

She took a deep breath. 'My laptop is in my car; I've written down all of the things that seem to have compromised the network. I'll go out and get it.'

'It's pouring.' Nat shook his head, determined to be a gentleman. 'You put the kettle on, and I'll go out and get it. Is your car locked?'

'No. The laptop is on the back seat in a leather case. Thank you.' A glimmer of the Nell of old came back.

He gestured to the cupboard above the sink. 'Cups and coffee are in that cupboard. Milk's in the fridge.' Nat figured if he gave her something to do, she might settle a bit more. 'I'll grab a brolly and be back in a minute.' He didn't look at her again before hurrying up the hall, but he did hear the cupboard open as he reached the front door. Nat picked up the umbrella that he'd left there earlier and ran down the steps and across the yard towards the gate.

The wind roared in from the sea, whipping the mango trees around the house into a frenzy; the rain was horizontal and stung his face. One tree had already come down near the gate, and he had to clamber over it. Waves crashed on the beach behind the house; the normally smooth water was churning like a washing machine. As he wrenched open the back door of Nell's car, a loud and ominous creak caught his attention. He swung around as a deafening crack came from around the back of the house. For a second he thought it was another lightning strike, but his mouth dropped open as a massive branch of the towering mango tree at the back of the laundry sheared off and fell onto the roof of the house.

'Shit!' He slammed the car door shut, forgetting all about the laptop in his haste to get to the house and Nell. The roof over the back of the house had collapsed and loose sheets of corrugated iron were lifting in the wind. As Nat ran across the yard, a sheet of iron sheared off with a loud screech. It blew along the side of the house, slicing open the side of the water tank before landing in the front yard. He ignored the water pouring out of the tank at the side of the house and raced up the stairs. He threw the umbrella on the porch and pushed the front door open.

'Nell,' he yelled. 'Nell, I'm coming.'

There was no answer and his blood ran cold. Only the sound of the wind and sea, and the continuing screeching of the flapping iron reached him. He raced down the hallway into a gust of cold wet wind. Above, live wires sizzled and snapped in the wind.

'Don't move,' he yelled racing back down the hall and out to the front porch. He turned off the power before running back to the kitchen. Hopefully, the battery backup had enough juice to keep his computers going, but that was the last of Nat's worries at the moment.

His passage was blocked by the end of the huge branch that had pierced a hole in the wall at the kitchen end of the hall. Heart thudding, he climbed over the thick branch, hands slipping on the wet bark. It was almost dark now.

'Nell, can you hear me?'

Nat pushed away the foliage that blocked his view as he carefully climbed over the branch that was wedged firmly across the kitchen and end of the hall.

Bloody hell. And into the computer room.

The branch had brought down the whole ceiling; he could see the sky through the huge gaping hole.

'Nell! For God's sake, where are you?'

Visions of her trapped beneath the huge branch filled his thoughts. 'Nell! Can you hear me?'

'I'm in here.' A faint voice came from the middle of the room.

'In where? Are you hurt?' He leaned forward and caught sight of her shoes sticking out beneath the kitchen table. He grabbed both sides of the table and with strength born of fear, lifted it above his head, moving it to the side of the room.

As his eyes adjusted to the dark, Nat could see Nell lying on the floor, her arms over her head. He reached down and gently touched her hands. 'Are you hurt?' He couldn't see any marks or blood anywhere, but that didn't mean the tree hadn't hit her when it came through the roof. 'Can you move, Nell?'

'Don't touch me.' She flinched at his touch.

He lowered his voice and spoke slowly. 'I have to get you out of here. I'm worried the rest of the roof will come down.'

'Don't touch me. I can get out myself.' As she spoke, she lowered her hands, and her eyes connected with his. Her face was pale, but he couldn't see if she'd been hurt.

'Don't move until I know you're okay. Did you hurt your back? Did the tree hit you?'

She shook her head. 'I'm all right. If you get out of my way, I'll get up.'

He held out his hand and this time her voice held anger.

'I told you, I'm all right. Don't touch me. Please.'

'All right, all right.' He stepped back with his hands raised. 'I'm just worried you're hurt.'

Despite Nell's assurances that she was okay, Nat could see her shaking as she rolled over and pushed herself to her feet.

She lifted her hand and gripped the side of the table. 'I heard the first crack and I dived under the table. I thought it was a lightning strike.' She inched along the table putting distance between them; as much as she could anyway with the huge branch filling the kitchen.

'No.' He looked up through the gaping hole in the ceiling. The wind had eased, and the rain had stopped. 'It was the mango tree out the back.'

'I can see it was a tree. It's a bit hard to miss.' Her voice was soft, but she forced a smile. White-faced, her hands shook as she reached up to push her hair back from her face. Enough to make him worry about her. For a moment, he caught another glimpse of the softness of the Nell of old; not this new hard woman she had become.

'Nell, I'm sorry this happened, but we need to get out now. We can get to the back door easily, but I need to know that you're okay first.'

'I'm all right. I'm not hurt.'

He nodded and held his hand out to help her over the branch, but she ignored it. With a shrug, Nat walked to the small landing at the top of the back steps and she followed him without another word. He watched to make sure she was telling the truth about being okay.

The branch had hit the side of the steps on its way down, and one of the posts halfway up had collapsed. Nat bit back a groan as the steps wobbled when he stood on the landing. There was a lot more damage to the house than he'd first thought. Not only the roof and the kitchen, and the water tank, not to mention the wiring; it looked like the structural integrity of his house had been compromised.

He couldn't bring myself to think what damage it had done to the equipment in the computer room. The room was next to the kitchen, and the roof over it had blown off. But until he got Nell out safely, Nat wasn't going to go and check it out.

'I'll go down first, and then when I get to the bottom, you come down after me. The stairs are a bit shaky.'

She nodded and Nat took off, jumping down the last three stairs. The staircase shook beneath his weight but held firm.

'Come on. If they collapse, jump and I'll catch you.' He held his arms out and could see the eye roll from where he stood.

It was only a matter of seconds before Nell had scurried down the stairs and they were both standing in the yard looking back at the house. The storm was moving inland quickly, and the sky had cleared. Brilliant stars began to appear in the night sky.

'What are you going to do? The house is a mess,' she asked softly. 'Do you rent? Or is it yours?'

If Nat didn't look at her, he could pretend that the concern came from the Nell he'd once known. He folded his arms and leaned back on the fence—the only part of the property that seemed to be intact. 'It was my grandparents' house. They left it to me. I moved up here just before Cyclone Debbie.' He uncrossed his arms and walked back towards the house. 'I can't believe the house survived that cyclone and that it only took a piddly storm like this to damage it.'

'I wouldn't call it a piddly storm.' Her voice was soft. 'I'm sorry your house is damaged. Do you have somewhere else to stay?'

'I haven't thought about that yet. We need to get you out of here though. I don't know what condition the road back to town will be in.'

'Look, I'll leave you to it. I'll drive back to Airlie Beach. I was going to anyway.'

'No, I'm not going to let you drive by yourself. The road could be blocked by more trees that have come down, and then you'll be stuck.' Nat frowned as thoughts whirled through his head. 'Come around to the front and wait near the gate, I just want to check something and get a couple of things. And please don't be tempted to drive off, because you'll leave me stranded. My car is in town getting fixed.'

He stared at her, surprised when she chuckled. 'The thought did cross my mind.'

'I thought it might have. Just give me a couple of minutes.'

Nat left Nell standing by the gate in the dark and headed for the front door.'

Chapter Six

Nell - 2010

'Nell, will you chill a bit! What in the bloody hell is wrong with you lately?' Pippa reached for the wine bottle and filled her glass to the top. They had spread a picnic rug in the park on the riverbank down the street from their flat.

'You've had enough.' Nell folded her arms and looked at Pippa with a scowl.

'Come on, you pair, stop fighting. We're supposed to be having a celebration picnic.' Tam reached for the bottle, topped her glass up and held it up to Nell.

'No, thank you.'

Tam shrugged and put it back in the chill pack, before lifting her glass. 'Well, here's to another year over.'

'And one closer to making our mark in the world.' Pippa squealed and took a slurp from her overflowing glass. She glanced across at Tam when Nell lay back on the grass and put her forearm over her eyes.

Nell knew they were both looking at her, but she didn't care. She was over this partying and being stupid most of the time. For goodness sake, they were almost twenty and should be taking their university studies more seriously. The spring sunshine was warm on her skin and she kept her eyes closed listening to her two friends talk.

'What's your plan for the long vacation, Tam?' Pippa's voice was always loud. Her clothes were always colourful and flamboyant, and it seemed as though she tried to match them with her voice and behaviour. She wanted to be seen, and that was the last thing that Nell wanted to do.

Nell tried to quell her growing irritation. It wasn't the girls' fault that she was a stick in the mud these days. She knew she should try harder, but some days it was hard enough to get out of bed. Her two besties were worried about her, but that was the least of her problems.

'I . . .um . . . have something to tell you,' Tam replied. 'Nell, are you awake? I want to tell you both at once.'

Nell rolled over and leaned on her elbows, resting her chin in her hands. 'Yes, I'm awake.'

'Tell us what?' Pippa said.

'I've decided to drop out.'

'What!' Nell sat up now and stared at Tam. How many times since last winter had she dreamed about doing the same thing? Leaving university, leaving Brisbane, leaving the girls behind and going somewhere new where she'd feel safe.

The problem was she didn't know where to go, nor could she afford it.

Tam cleared her throat. 'I've been offered an apprenticeship at Peppers. And they are going to pay for my course.' Her eyes lit up with excitement. 'Not at TAFE, but a private course that fast-tracks me and puts me with some of the top chefs in the country.'

'Here in Brisbane?' Nell's voice was quiet.

'No, Peppers by the Surf. Down at Surfers Paradise, and the problem is, it means letting you both down. I'm going to have to move down there and give up my room in the house.'

'How did that happen, Tam?' Nell asked quietly.

'Well, you know how I've been working as a kitchen hand at night in the city?'

Nell nodded.

'I've been doing a bit of preparation for the entrees there, and I impressed one of the chefs with something I suggested one night. He took it up and added it to the menu and it was a hit. Chad's moved down to Peppers and he put my name up for a traineeship. He knows that my dream is to be a chef. So to cut to the chase, I've had two interviews and I was offered the traineeship this morning.'

'Who's this Chad?' Nell asked.

Tam ignored her question. 'And it's great timing, because I've got two years of my degree behind me, and I'll defer, and I can go back and finish externally in a year or two if I want to.'

'Who's this guy?' Nell repeated. 'He seems to know more about you than we do. *I* didn't know you wanted to be a chef.'

'Me either. I just thought you liked to cook,' Pippa said.

'Well, I always have.' Tam said quietly. 'I just didn't share it with anyone. 'I guess I thought it didn't have the prestige of going to uni and getting a degree.'

'Oh, shit. Where are we going to get a third at this end of the uni year?' Pippa huffed.

'I know. I feel bad, but I might have someone for you. Have you seen Nat, lately, Nell?' Tam asked.

Nell froze, but she kept her voice even. 'Nat who?'

'God, you know who I mean. That cutie, Nat Dwyer, the guy who goes to lectures with you.'

'No, I haven't seen him, but what about him?'

Since that night last winter before "it" happened, Nell had avoided everyone. She made sure she got to lectures late and sat in the back row of the lecture theatre near the door and was the first to leave. A few times at the beginning she had seen Nat turn around and look for her, but she'd pretended not to see him. It was hard enough sitting next to anyone, let alone a guy.

'I know he's looking for a room. I heard he lost his place in the residential hall.'

'I heard that, 'Pip said. 'Too many parties and he got caught with a couple of girls in his room after curfew one night. I'm sure it was innocent.'

Tam and Pippa exchanged a glance and burst out laughing, but Nell pursed her lips and looked away.

'Oh, God, we'll miss you, Tam,' Pip said. 'But thanks for suggesting Nat. Nell, can you tell him the room's available when you see him at lectures?'

'No!' Nell knew her voice was unnecessarily loud, but she stared back at them.

'Why so adamant?' Tam frowned at her. 'I thought you were mates, aren't you?'

'No, he's just someone I used to sit with in lectures. I hardly know him.'

'Used to?' Damn, she'd slipped up there and Pippa picked straight up on it. 'Why used to?'

'We've changed majors.'

'Well, I vote we offer it to him. We can't afford to split the rent two ways, Nell. And it'll go up after the long vacation too. It always does.'

'No. I don't want to share with a guy. I don't want to have to worry about wandering out in a towel or running out to the laundry to get my knickers out of the dryer. But most of all, I don't want Nat Dwyer. He'd have a different girl in there every night. You know what he's like.'

'You're being too hard, Nell. He's no worse than any other guy on campus.'

'No. No guys. Please.' She looked past the confused looks on Tam and Pippa's faces. A CityCat was cruising silently up the river, and the ducks that had been on the edge of the grass took off with raucous honks. 'All the guys on campus are like that, so we'll have another girl, thank you. Otherwise, I go too.'

'All right,' Tam conceded, reluctance in her voice. 'You'll have to find someone then. I don't want to go through this every time I come up with a name.'

'I will.' Nell pushed herself to her feet and tucked her black T-shirt into her khaki pants. 'I've got to be somewhere. I'll see you both later.'

She knew that Tam and Pippa stared at her as she strode off. Okay, she felt bad, but she couldn't help it. These days she didn't care what anyone thought about her.

Even her best friends.

Chapter Seven

Nell, 2020

Nell sighed while she waited for Nat to come out of the house. Her hands were shaking, but the close call when that blasted tree had come through the ceiling had at least taken away the fear of being in the house with him. Even though it had given her one hell of a fright.

If she'd known the business was run from a private house, she would never have come this far.

But really, she didn't have a choice; she would have come because she had to get the problem fixed. She was caught between a rock and a hard place; there was no way Nell would let Pippa down, so she had to get someone to fix the network, and Nat was the only local someone. She leaned back against the car, her thoughts in turmoil as she looked up at the sky.

It was hard to believe that there had been such a violent storm a short time ago. The wind had gone, and the sky was full of stars; even the noise of the sea had abated. As she stared out over the sea her phone trilled in her pocket.

She glanced at the screen and answered. 'Hey, Pip.'

'Nell. Where are you? I just wanted to check you didn't get caught in that freak storm that roared over us and towards the coast.'

'I'm fine. Just a bit of wind and rain. Is everything okay out there?' She gripped the phone and frowned.

'Yeah, there was a lot of thunder and lightning, but no damage, thank goodness. Rafe heard the storm warning, and we got the outdoor furniture away in the bar just in time. A couple of trees blew down, but nothing near the house or the huts. Where are you?'

'Um, I'm just at the networking . . . um. . . place, and then heading back to Airlie Beach.'

'Okay, that's good then. The other thing I wanted to tell you was Jiminy's coming to the island tomorrow late morning, so if the time suits you, jump on his boat. If it doesn't, ring me, and I'll come and get you whenever you're ready.'

'That should work out okay with me. I'll probably get the early ferry over. If there's anything you want, text me a list and I'll pick it up at Hamo. What's Jiminy doing?'

'Okay, I'll ask Tam, and I'll text you. We've got another staff member arriving tomorrow. He's bringing her over.'

'Who's that?'

'Tam's friend—the one from the Gold Coast.'

The door to the house banged shut, and Nat walked across to the gate, his keys jangling in his hand.

'Okay, sounds good. I have to go. See you tomorrow.' Nell disconnected before Pip could ask any more questions.

'Thanks for waiting,' Nat said, but as he looked back at the house his lips were set, and his brow wrinkled

'What's wrong?' she asked. 'Apart from your caved-in roof, I mean.'

'There's a fair bit of damage inside. There's no power now and my backup system didn't come on, so I've got no computer system going. The room copped a fair bit of rain. I've covered it up as best I could, but I don't think I'll be working from there for a while. I took some photos and I'll have to get onto my insurance company.'

For the first time, Nell noticed he was carrying a case, and a backpack slung over his shoulder.

'I brought my laptop and some clothes and stuff. Hopefully, I can help you out.'

Nell went to the driver's side to open the door, but Nat walked around beside her. She took a step back, wondering what he wanted.

'Um, Nell? How would you feel about me driving your car?'

She shrugged. 'It's not my car. It's a hire car. I don't care. You probably know the road better.'

'And you can tell me what's wrong with your computer system as we travel. Where did you hire the car?'

'Port of Airlie, where the ferry from Hamilton Island comes in.'

'Okay. I've got a mate with a two-bedroom unit at the Mantra near there. Once we get there, we can grab something to eat, and I can try to log into your network remotely and have a look around. If that suits you?'

Nell hesitated. She knew she couldn't afford to be precious, but—

He glanced across at her as he turned the car. Just like she'd thought it would, it took Nat about six goes to turn it around.

'I'm happy to look at the network together, but I'll find my own accommodation and dinner.'

He shrugged 'Suit yourself. The apartment's free.'

She didn't answer and there was no more talk as Nat concentrated on the narrow dirt road. Night had fallen and velvety darkness surrounded them as the headlights picked out the lonely road ahead. Eventually, they reached an intersection and he turned right onto a bitumen road.

'Okay, we're on the main road now. We've got half an hour or so for you to tell me about the setup you have and then tell me what problems you're having.'

Nell cleared her throat, ill at ease. She didn't know the right language to use to an expert. 'Okay. I'll keep it simple. I've set up one more powerful computer in the office to run the various software packages we use, rather than installing them on the individual laptops that we use in other places around the resort.'

He nodded. 'Good. What networking software are you using?'

'Um, I'm not sure what you mean.'

His voice was patient. 'Okay, are you PC based or is it an Apple Network?'

'PC. Windows, I mean.'

'And the proprietary software to set up your network?'

'I'm not sure.' Heat ran up Nell's neck and she was pleased it was dark in the car. 'Maybe we're better off waiting until you can log in and look.'

'Let me explain, and you might know what I mean. The hardware that you'll be using will be on the server—that is the backend computer you described to me—the clients, that is, your laptops, and the transmission medium, and connecting devices. The software components are the operating system and protocols that make them all talk to each other.'

'Yes, I understand that, but I don't know the name of what I'm using to put it all together.'

'Okay, not a problem. I'll see when I log in. Tell me a bit about the resort and what you're using the network to do.'

Finally, a question she could answer. Nell relaxed and settled into her seat more comfortably. She hadn't realised how tense she'd been holding herself.

The wheels hummed on the bitumen, interrupted by an occasional splash as they hit puddles on the road as she outlined the accounting software, the reservations system and the ordering system on Tam's laptop in the kitchen.

'Good, sounds simple and effective.'

'There's one thing I need more than anything, Nat. That's why I came over to the mainland today.'

'What's that?' Nat changed back a gear and they slowed down. 'Meets all your needs?'

'What are you doing?' Nell shot an anxious glance across the car. 'Where are you going?'

He looked at her briefly and his brow furrowed in a frown. 'I'm looking out for the turn-off to Cannonvale. It's hard to see in the dark between the sugar cane fields. The signpost blew down a couple of storms back and they haven't replaced it yet. You can't see the road until you're just about at the turnoff.'

'Cannonvale?' Her voice was a squeak. 'Why are we going to Cannonvale?'

The car picked up speed again, and Nat's voice was firm, yet patient. 'Because we go through Cannonvale to get to Airlie Beach, and then on to Port of Airlie.' A road came up on the left and he quickly indicated and took the turn. 'This is it now.'

'Oh, sorry, I've only been to the mainland once before. We usually only go from the island to Hamilton for anything we need. Our supplies and stuff come across on the barge and then we pick it up. Pippa—or the resort, I suppose— has a launch that's big enough to take a fair bit onboard.' Nell tried to take a deep breath and relax but her whole body was tight. Conversation was hard. She hadn't been this close to—or alone with— a man in ten years.

'What was the one thing you need?'

'I need this problem fixed now. Not later this week or next week. The first part of the resort is opening next week, and I must have the network up and running. I have to be able to access the bookings that I've lost.' Her voice dropped. 'And Tam's orders and the rest of the data I've backed up.'

'Okay. If you can give me half the morning tomorrow to get my insurance sorted and collect my car, I'll probably be able to come over tomorrow. Would that suit?

'Oh God, yes.' Relief zoomed in and she leaned her head back on the headrest.

'I have to go out to Hamo. I've got a few jobs out there that I have to touch base on.' He shook his head ruefully. 'The way my computer system was looking, I think I'll be doing a lot of onsite jobs in the next little while.'

'Thank you,' she breathed out quietly.

'Nellie? I mean Nell. Can I say something to you? I'd like to clear the air before I start working with you.'

'Y … es,' she said slowly. Nerves were skittering all through her. Her stomach was churning, her fingers were aching, and it was hard to swallow. Her skin tingled as though there was an army of ants marching over it. She tried to close her eyes and visualise something pleasant. She'd learned that strategy from a YouTube clip on anxiety attacks. That's the closest she'd ever got to counselling.

Something pleasant. Take a breath, close your eyes and think of something you love to do. A place where you feel safe, calm and happy. The words ran through her head and she let her imagination conjure up a happy picture.

Sitting on the beach at Pentecost Island watching the sun go down, with the girls. A bottle or two of bubbles, lots of laughter, lots of happiness. Except for the night Eliza had almost drowned, but that had turned out okay. Her eyes flew open as Nat spoke again, interrupting her meditation.

'I want to say sorry.'

She turned her head slowly to look at him. He was gripping the steering wheel, his attention fixed on the road ahead.

'Sorry for what?' Her words sounded husky to her ears, but over the stupid buzzing that nerves had kicked off, it was hard to tell if the huskiness was real or not. Nell cleared her throat and said it again. 'For what?'

'For that time I came to your office at the Gold Coast and was really rude to you when I left. It bothered me for ages afterwards. I'm sorry, it was an awful thing to say and I didn't mean it. I lashed out at you, and I had no right to. I was rude and cruel, and you didn't deserve that.' He shook his head as he stared at the road ahead.

'I did.' Heat filled Nell's face and she looked straight ahead. 'It was eight years ago. And I goaded you into it. I was in a bad place then, and I'm sorry. I said some rude things too.'

'Okay then. Apologies exchanged and accepted. I'm cool with that, are you?'

She nodded.

'Can I ask you one more thing? It's something else that's bothered me since we were at uni. Maybe I'll need to apologise again.'

Nell closed her eyes; she knew what was coming, but for some unknown reason, she felt safe, cocooned in the car with Nat. Safer than she had for a long time, listening to his gentle voice as the wheels humming on the bitumen soothed her, and the dark of the night closed everything else out. It was as though they were in a different world, and what had shaped her into the person she was now receded.

'What did I do to make you hate me so much, Nellie? I went down to the bar the night that *Cat Empire* was playing. The night we sat together for the last time in that lecture hall. Was it because you thought I was playing with you? Going to lead you on? Treat you like the playboy I was supposed to be treated others? It wasn't true you know.'

The first tear that plopped onto her hand surprised Nell. She lifted her hand and looked at the damp spot. Turning her hand around slowly she rubbed her eyes, and then took a long shuddering breath in.

'I'm sorry that it worried you so much, Nat. It wasn't you. It wasn't about you. It never was. Something happened that night and I've never got over it.' Her voice fell to a whisper. 'I've never told another soul what happened. I was so ashamed, and I blamed myself. I've never even told the girls. I thought if I didn't tell anyone I could forget it and it wouldn't be real.'

'The girls? You mean Pippa and Tam? You lived with them, didn't you?'

'Yes, I did. What happened was all my fault. I'm sorry that you thought you'd done something. For months afterwards, I didn't give anyone else a thought. It was all me and it was all my fault. I brought it on myself. The way I'd dressed, and the confidence I had. I thought I was invincible, and the world was at my feet.'

'You were a hell of a lot of fun to sit with in lectures. I used to look forward to those subjects.'

'Thank you. After that night, I lost a lot of trust and all my self-confidence. That's why I sat by myself in lectures and spent the rest of the time in the apartment I shared with Pippa. Tam moved out, and it was just the two of us. I didn't want anyone else there, so I scrounged and paid two shares of the rent. I told Pippa I was studying, but most of the time I sat in my room or slept.'

'Depression?' Nat's tone was kind. 'I'm no stranger to that. My sister had a breakdown in her teens.'

'In hindsight, yes. I was young and stupid. And like I said I thought I was invincible.'

'Will you tell me what happened? Maybe it would help to talk about it?'

Nell felt as though she was in a dream state. Was she really sitting in a car with Nat Dwyer? Was she really about to tell him what had happened to her?

Chapter Eight

Nell, 2010

The students from the lecture hall jostled at the entrance and Nell soon lost sight of Nat in the crowd. For a moment she stood looking at the spot where she'd last seen him.

It would be great if Nat came down to the bar. A happy warm feeling settled in Nell's chest and she headed outside into the colder night. The way he'd looked at her was different tonight; it was as though he noticed her for the first time.

Winter was around the corner and she pulled her bright red cardigan around her shoulders. Her dress was short, and her legs were bare; she hadn't thought about how cool it would be tonight when she'd got dressed for lectures in the warm autumn morning.

Before she'd left the apartment, she'd slipped on a dress and shoes that would do for both the lecture and dancing in the bar afterwards. She was really looking forward to having a few drinks and letting her hair down with the girls. Uni was great and having Tam and Pippa on the same campus meant good times most nights of the week. They'd been friends since primary school; she and Tam had been over the moon when Pippa moved back to Brisbane to go to the same uni. They were all doing different courses and they'd found a cheap house to share over at Bardon. The ferry terminal at Milton wasn't too much of a walk from the house.

There was always something on at the uni bar, but *Cat Empire* was going to be awesome tonight. She just hoped they had come on late as most bands seemed to. What rotten luck that it was tonight of all nights when they'd had to go to that boring lecture.

A southerly change had come roaring in while they'd been in the lecture, and now the wind was whistling through the tall gums along the riverfront. At least it would be warm down in the student union . . . once she was inside. And a few wines would soon warm her up; she just hoped that Tam and Pippa hadn't got too much of a head start.

Nell shivered and paused outside the building. Most of the students were heading towards the car park, but she'd caught the CityCat to uni this morning, so she was going to have to walk down to the bar. She stood there and tapped her fingers on the side of her thigh and looked around, deciding which was the best way to go.

Two choices.

The long way along the path that wound through the campus, and led to the front of the bar, or the shortcut that she took up from the ferry terminal at the river every morning. There was a path halfway along that shortcut that led down to the bar. There'd been rumours of a couple of assaults there over the past year, but she put it down to the usual gossip that circulated. It was always someone who told someone who told someone else.

Nell hesitated as she looked at the path. It would be dark, but it would be so much quicker. The campus was big, and the shortcut would save her at least fifteen minutes in the cold wind, and that was fifteen minutes extra she could listen to the band. And fifteen minutes sooner that she could start partying. She stood there for a moment considering her options and as she waited, the faint sound of the band drifted across from the other side of the campus, enticing her. A shiver ran up Nell's back as the wind whistled through the gap in the buildings, and that decided her.

With a confident nod, she held her book and bag close to her chest and took off towards the path that was almost hidden between the trees.

Nell was focused on meeting up with Tam and Pippa and she didn't notice the figure standing in the shadows at the side of the building.

She only had fifty metres before she reached the student union building when it happened.

"It"—the event that would change her confidence and define her new personality overnight. In the months and the years that followed, she always remembered that night as the catalyst for changing the Nell of "before" into the Nell of "after".

As she hurried past the Law building, and into the narrow corridor that led to the bar, a rustle in the shrubs behind her sent her heart rate up a notch. She glanced behind her and a fleeting shadow brushed against the side of the building near the steps that went into the foyer.

It was just the wind moving the trees, she told herself.

But her heart was in her throat and when she heard footsteps behind her, Nell knew she was in trouble. She took a deep breath and started to run, but before she could get away, a strong hand gripped her arm. She didn't even have time to pull out the pepper spray she always carried.

Before she knew it, she was on her knees and was being dragged into the shrubbery at the side of the building.

He didn't say one word to her the whole time.

Her assailant's other hand moved to her face and covered her mouth and nose. She tried to scream, but the hand pressed hard against her lips. An overpowering smell of dirt and car oil made her gag.

'Please, don't hurt me,' she tried to whimper, but no sound came out. Something cold and sharp touched her neck and stars dotted her vision.

##

It was only a few minutes later, but it seemed like a long time had passed before he left her huddled in the wet leaves of the garden next to that building. A couple of guys had walked down the dark path, talking and laughing and her assailant had put his hand over her mouth again so she couldn't call out. She'd lain there with her eyes closed, trying not to make a sound as the knife pressed against her neck.

He must have been worried that they would come back because he'd shoved her away and taken off. Her handbag was gone, and a thin trickle of blood was running down her neck where the knife had nicked her skin when she'd tried to move. Before the men had walked past, he'd pushed her dress up above her waist and her knickers had twisted.

Nell knew it could have been a lot worse if he hadn't left her, but her hands and legs were shaking so much she couldn't move. He had intended to sexually assault her; he'd pressed against her just before the two guys had almost come upon them.

Her heart pounded in time with the deep throb of the music from the bar close by.

Footsteps crunched on the path nearby and she froze.

What if he came back?

Maybe he'd opened her purse and seen how little was in there. Maybe he'd decided to finish what—

It started to rain as she pushed herself to her feet; one of those heavy tropical Brisbane showers that could soak you in two minutes and then stop as suddenly as it began. She rearranged her knickers, so they weren't cutting into her, pulled her dress down and smoothed her shaking hands over it. Hurrying out to the main path she joined the throng of students who were drinking on the ground-level covered veranda.

Pushing herself into the middle of the crowd, she let the sweaty bodies press against her until she felt warm again.

##

'What did you do to your neck, Nell?' Pippa had spotted her when she and Tam had come out of the bar between songs. 'It's bleeding.' Pippa reached down into her bra and pulled a tissue out. 'It's clean.'

'I . . . I . . . ran into a tree when it was raining. I fell over.' Shame filled Nell and she swore that no one, not even her best friends would ever know what had happened. She swallowed and forced her voice to stop shaking. 'Would you believe I've lost my bag. Can you give me your key, please Pip? I'm going home. I'm soaked.'

'Aw, come on, Nell. The band's fantastic. You've been waiting for them for ages. Come and dance.' Pippa tried to pull her into the bar, but Nell stood firm.

'No. I want to go home. I don't feel well.'

'Okay, party pooper.' Pippa dug into her jeans pocket and produced her key to the small flat they shared over in Milton.

'Can you lend me five bucks for the bus? I lost my purse too.'

Tamsin narrowed her eyes and zoomed in close to her face. Both girls had obviously had a few beers and it was dark outside. 'You okay, love?'

'I'm fine. It was a shit lecture. I got wet. I fell over. I lost my bag. Are you satisfied? I'm not in the mood to party. I just want to go home to bed.' Her teeth were chattering from cold and shock

Tamsin nodded and Pippa shrugged as she handed over a handful of gold coins.

The band started up again, and the two girls squealed as they ran back into the bar. 'We'll see you at home.'

By the time Tamsin and Pippa arrived home after midnight, with much noise and hilarity, Nell was in bed in her room pretending to be asleep. She'd stood under the shower for half an hour until she stopped shaking and then collapsed into bed.

***

Nat pulled the car over as soon as they reached town. 'God, Nell. You never told anyone? You didn't report it?'

'No. I was too ashamed. And it didn't matter. Because he assaulted another girl in the same spot a few days later, and she screamed blue murder, and he was caught.'

'I remember that.' He looked at her and his face was shadowed inside the car. 'He was charged with a few counts of sexual assault and went to jail.'

'He did. I followed the case, day by day, and I thought that I'd start to feel better when it was all over. He got a long time because the last charge was attempted murder too.' She sniffed. 'But I didn't. It set me back even further, thinking that he could have raped and killed me that night. I lost my confidence. In everything. I didn't want it to happen again. The sensible part of me tells me it was a random attack, and I was lucky he was interrupted, and he didn't—' she drew in a long shuddering breath. 'I stopped wearing dresses and anything colourful. I just wanted to blend in and be a nobody.'

'Oh, Nellie, you could never be a nobody.'

'Thank you, Nat. But it's what I wanted to be. The last few months on the island have given me a lot more confidence. I'm gradually getting more confident when there are men around, but it's taken me a long time. Pippa has a partner, Rafe, and we've had another man, a French sailor helping out on the island for a few weeks.'

'Bloody ten years of your life, Nell. Did you ever go to counselling to try and work through it?

She shook her head. 'No, because I was too ashamed. Like I said I didn't tell anyone. I could have gone to the police when he was arrested. He might have got an even longer sentence, but I just couldn't.' Tears began to run down her face again and her throat clogged. 'I don't know why I told you, Nat. You'll think even less of me now.'

'Never, Nell. Please don't think that.' Nat hesitated and then lifted one hand from the steering wheel and reached over and squeezed her hand briefly. 'I feel very honoured that you trusted me enough to tell me about that night.' He turned his attention to her for a fleeting second and she held his gaze.

Even though it was dim in the car, she could see the determination in his eyes.

'And I'm going to do whatever I can to help you heal.' He squeezed her hand again. 'Friends?'

She nodded. 'Yes, Nat. Friends.'

Chapter Nine

Nell

'Are you sure you want to get your own room?' Nat said as they turned at the roundabout into the Port of Airlie. 'My mate's is a freebie.'

'Yes,' Nell said softly. 'I'd be more comfortable. Please don't take it personally, it's just me. And besides, I don't have to pay for it. Pippa said all the costs of this trip can come out of the company.'

'Not a problem,' Nat said kindly. 'Just offering.'

He'd called his mate before they pulled back onto the road at Cannonvale and got the code to collect the security card to get into the unit. Nell had composed herself as Nat approached the turn to park in the private and gated car park beneath the multi-story building.

'Wait.' She swallowed and held her hand up. 'If you don't mind a short walk, drive over and park it over in the rental car park and I'll do the paperwork in the morning before I catch the ferry back. It will be . . .um . . . easier.'

'Good idea. I wasn't sure if I remembered the code for the car park anyway. I forgot to ask Brent for it.'

'You've stayed here before?' she asked.

'Yeah, Brent and his family live over on Hamo and he keeps this unit for when they come to the mainland. He's one of my clients. He's got a couple of businesses over there. And a house and the kids go to school on the island.'

'I heard you do some work at Hamilton. It's a fair way for you to go from your place.'

Nat nodded as he parked the car. 'I stay on Hamo sometimes because I have a dozen or so clients over there now. It's the biggest part of my business, that's why I wasn't keen on taking the job down at Proserpine. I think he wanted a cut of the business. And yes, it's a pain getting down from Hydeaway Bay and catching the ferry across as often as I have to. Brent offered me this unit at a good rate, but I said no because I know he and his family use it pretty often.'

'You haven't thought about living over on the islands?'

He smiled ruefully. 'That would be ideal, but the rent over there is too high. Maybe when I build my business up a bit more, I might be able to consider it.' He opened the back door of the hire car and took the two laptops and his backpack out while Nell retrieved her overnight bag from the boot. After clicking the remote he handed the keys over.

'Thanks. I'll go to reception and book a room for the night.'

Nat walked towards reception with her. 'I'll wait until you know you can get a room for sure, and then I thought we might grab something to eat and we can work over dinner. How do you feel about that?'

Nell stepped through the door into the foyer when he held it open. 'Thank you. Yes, that's sounds good.'

##

It didn't take long to organise a one-bedroom unit and as luck would have it, it was on the same floor in the north wing along the corridor from the one that Nat stayed in. They caught the lift up together.

'I've booked a table in the fish and chip place for seven-thirty. Does that give you enough time?'

Nell glanced at her watch. 'Yes, thank you. I'll see you down there.' As he walked away, she put the key card over the security sensor. When it clicked open, she called him. 'Nat?'

'Yes.' He paused a short way along the corridor.

'Thank you.' She stepped into the apartment and closed the door before he could reply. The first thing that caught her eye was the glittering lights of the marina below. Walking slowly through the apartment, Nell put her bag on the king-size bed before she pushed open the doors and stepped onto the small balcony. The air was fresh and held a hint of a tropical spice from the trees that formed a privacy screen between her balcony and the next. She slipped her shoes off and wandered into the kitchen and opened the fridge. There were a couple of small bottles of bubbles in there and she took one out and reached for a glass before she headed back out onto the verandah. She pulled a second chair out and put her feet up before she popped the top of the bottle. The bubbles fizzed over the side of her glass.

She yawned; it had been a big day and it seemed like more than one day had passed since Pippa had dropped her off at Hamo this morning to catch the ferry.

Things hadn't turned out too badly after all.

Apart from the storm, and the damage it had done to Nat's house. He was a kind and gentle guy—just like he had been at uni—and she was feeling more at ease in male company than she had for a very long time.

Sometimes, she had to force herself to relax when Rafe and Phillipe joined them in the bar on the island.

Talking to Nat had been cathartic and an unfamiliar lightness relaxed her. She sat on the balcony for half an hour watching the people walk along the edge of the water and listening to the happy voices that drifted up. Someone turned some music on below, and she jumped up realising how much time had passed; she had to get tidy and meet Nat at the restaurant.

Nell unpacked the small overnight bag and pulled a face when she pulled out the spare pair of khaki pants and a clean T-shirt. Maybe it was time to break her habits.

She knew when Matt looked at her that it wasn't what she wore that made her the person she was. Clothes weren't important; it was what was within and she knew he would have treated her exactly the same polite way if she'd been wearing a dress. The hang-up was all hers.

Nell was thoughtful as she jumped in and took a quick shower in the luxurious bathroom. Tam and Pippa had been on her back for ages, and on very rare occasions they had got her into a dress. After dressing in her clean clothes, she quickly dried her hair and reached for her red lipstick. Hesitating she stared at herself in the mirror and held the lipstick up.

After "it" had happened, she used the red lipstick as a deliberate reminder about how she looked and the image that she presented in the world. After a few years, it just became a habit. Slowly, Nell put the red lipstick back into her toiletries bag without opening the case.

A relaxed face stared back at her as she pinched her cheeks and pulled her hair back into a scrunchie. Her cheeks were pink with a healthy glow. Her eyes were bright, and she felt light, and confident that Nat was going to be able to solve her network problem, and she wouldn't have to worry any more about putting the resort opening in jeopardy.

Nat sounded as though he knew what he was talking about, although that shouldn't be a surprise. Even before he'd finished his degree, he'd been a whiz at that stuff, and now he had ten years in business under his belt. She wondered if he could fix the problem remotely, but she doubted it.

No, I'm getting ahead of myself.

She'd wait until he had a look downstairs after they'd eaten. With a rare smile, Nell picked up her laptop and closed the unit door behind her and headed down to the concourse where the fish and chip restaurant overlooked the marina.

##

Nat hadn't come down to the restaurant yet, and Nell waited at the counter until the waitress was free to take her over to a table overlooking the water. She unpacked her laptop and turned it on, taking the opportunity to use the local Wi-Fi to check her email. When she'd cleared her email, she decided to see if she could log onto the resort network remotely before Nat arrived.

Nell bit her lip and waited for the usual disconnect thirty seconds after her password was accepted.

She waited and counted and sure enough, she was disconnected before she reached thirty. With a sigh, she closed the lid and reached for her water glass as Nat

65

walked across to the table. His hair was damp, and he'd changed his clothes.

'Sorry, I had a few calls to make. I was trying to sort out the insurance on my house and my computers,' he said as she sat across from her.

'What will you do? You won't be able to live in the house, will you? The kitchen is demolished, and half the roof came down.'

'Yeah, that's right. Nat ran his hand through his damp hair. 'I'll talk to my mate and maybe stay down here for a few days, but I'll see how we go trying to log into your network before I make any calls or decisions. I've got a couple of jobs out on Hamilton Island so if I need to come out and look at your physical setup, I'll fit that in in the next day or so.'

Nat caught the attention of the waitress as she walked past the table. Nell was sipping on a glass of water. He gestured to the drink menu. 'Would you like a drink before we eat?'

Her lips tilted in a smile. 'I'll admit to a quick drink on the balcony before I got changed.' She thought for a moment and then nodded. 'Why not? After the day we've had, I think we deserve one tonight.' She knew her smile was tentative, but she got a wide grin back from Nat.

'I think we do too. Wine?' He raised his eyebrows as he held up the menu.

She nodded. 'Yes, you choose.'

Nell watched as Nat quickly perused the wines on offer. His hair shone from the soft light above them, and a slight frown wrinkled his brow as he concentrated. His face was as familiar to her now as it had been ten years ago. Finally, he chose, and the waitress nodded.

'I won't be long. Perhaps you'd like to look at the food menu while you wait. We're going to get busy in the next little while. If you get your order in before that big table, your meals will come out a lot quicker.'

Nat looked up and held Nell's gaze. 'How does that sound to you? If we eat first, we can focus on your laptop after?'

She quickly agreed. 'Sounds good to me. I'm a bit hungry. It's been a long time since lunch at Proserpine.'

Nat grinned back and her tummy did a funny little jump as she noticed the familiar dimple in his left cheek.

'I was going to offer you a biscuit with the cuppa we were going to have,' he said.

'Before the roof blew into your kitchen,' she said with a laugh before she killed the smile. 'Sorry, that was really rude. It's not a laughing matter.'

Nat flicked a dismissive wave. 'Might as well look on the bright side.'

Their eyes met and held, and Nell started to hum the tune from the Monty Python movie they'd both loved.

Nat chuckled loudly and a few heads turned to look at them 'How many times did you sing that to me in lectures when we got bored shitless?'

'Lots. Mainly in McMinn's. Remember him?'

'How could I forget? Hours and hours of my life—our lives—never to be gotten back.' He held her gaze a little bit longer until Nell dropped her eyes. She felt uncomfortable and kept her head down as she twisted her hands in her lap.

Why on earth did I let my guard down and hum that silly song? He must think I'm an idiot, she thought.

'But he chuckled,' a little voice inside told her. 'Nat's a good guy. One of the really good ones and you are being way too hard on him.'

Heat suffused her face and she pulled her laptop over to try to focus on what they were there for.

What she was here for. No other reason.

'I managed to log in, but the connection dropped out like it usually does,' Nell said firmly. 'It wasn't the Wi-Fi here because I cleared my email first.'

'Boot it up then, and I'll take a quick look while we wait for the waitress to come back. But have a look at the menu first.'

'I know what I want. Fish and chips will be fine for me,' she said as the laptop started up with a whir. 'This is how I get into the network when I'm off-site.' She half-turned the laptop so Nat could see it and craned her neck so she could point to the screen and see what she was doing.

'It's hard to see the screen with the laptop at that angle. Do you mind if I come around to your side of the table and have a look?' Nat asked.

'No, of course not.' She knew her voice was a little hesitant, but she appreciated his consideration and moved her chair further to the left. Nat stood and brought his chair around next to hers, and she moved away a little bit further.

Calm down. He's a good guy. Nell repeated that over and over as Nat's knee brushed against her bare leg. It was all she could do not to get up and run.

But she soon found she needn't have worried as Nat was totally focused on the screen in front of them. After a few minutes he seemed to forget that she was even sitting next to him. Nell leaned back in her chair and let her gaze run over him as he clicked keys and looked at her screen. A waft of something fresh and citrusy drifted over to her. His chinos and shirt were perfectly pressed, and she wondered if he'd ironed them before he'd come down.

Nell looked down at her wrinkled shirt and shorts and knew she needed to make more of an effort from now on. Nothing to do with Nat, but it was time to stop this silly obsession with drab clothes and bland colours. Spilling her story to him had been a wakeup call, and she felt like she'd woken from a long sleep. From now on things would be different; it was time to get herself out of the introverted state she'd been in for way too long.

Nell nodded as she came to a decision, but embarrassment flooded through her; she lifted her head and was surprised to find Nat looking at her intently.

Chapter Ten

'Was I talking to myself?' Nell asked.

'Um. No? Were you?' He frowned. 'But I think I've found your problem.'

'Already?'

'Well, one of the problems anyway. Some of the codes in the back-end need work. But it looks like the main problem is your physical set-up I'll have to come out to your resort.' Nat closed the laptop and Nell relaxed as he moved his chair around to his side of the table. 'I thought I'd have to look at your set-up. This was a long shot at trying something to trick it into letting me stay logged in,' he said as he reached for the carafe of water on the table.

'I thought you might.' Nell bit her lip as she thought of the bar opening that was getting closer by the day. 'I hate to ask you this after all that's happened to your house, but do you think there's any chance you could come out tomorrow?'

'Maybe. I'll have to make some calls. How do you get there? Do you have a boat service to the island for your guests?'

Nell shook her head. 'We're not open yet, but I know Pippa is looking into that. One of her friends has a charter business that takes passengers to the outlying islands. Apparently, there used to be more resorts on other islands, but there's not many left now. I have to meet Jiminy at the marina at noon.'

'Jiminy?' Nat's eyes lit up. 'That's an unusual name. It has to be my mate from Hamo.'

'You know him?'

'Yeah, he's a little bit older than me. I spent a lot of time up at my grandparents' place in my teens.' He chuckled. 'Mum was working fulltime, and she didn't trust me at home alone. I was a bit of a wild one in those days, so I got packed off to the islands to be babysat. It was great. I had more freedom with my grandparents than I'd ever had. But I stayed out of trouble up here. There was so much to do.'

'Did you live in the house at Dingo Beach with them?'

'I did. I met Jiminy when I was learning to sail. He lived at Dingo in those days too and he had an old sailing boat that I helped him do up. We'd sail and camp on the islands. I know Pentecost. We used to go rock climbing there.'

'Sounds like you had a great time.'

'I did. It was really hard to go back to the city at the end of the school holidays. Then I didn't come up much when I started uni, and then both my grandparents passed before I finished my degree.' He looked at her with a sad smile. 'As you know, I spent some time down at the Goldie, but it was way too hectic for me. I packed up and started my own business up here when I inherited the house.'

'And it's going okay?'

'I'm slowly building it up. I've picked up quite a bit of business on Hamo, and the word is spreading.' He shook his head. 'The damage from that storm is going to set me back a bit though.'

'Well, I appreciate your expertise. And I'm pleased you can come out to have a look. I'm at my wit's end. I really need it fixed. I don't want to let Pippa down.'

'Okay, I don't think there will be too much of a problem. If you can give me a couple of hours in the morning to sort out my house and my insurance and get some stuff happening there, I'll grab the eleven o'clock ferry with you and come out.'

'Do you have any idea how long it will take to fix?'

'I won't know until I look at your network. It could be a couple of hours, or it could mean reloading all of your network software, looking at your Wi-Fi and then it could take another couple of days.'

'Oh.' Disappointment shot through Nell.

'If it does take longer, is there anywhere where I can stay overnight on the island?'

'I'm sure we can find room for you. We've got another new staff member coming out with Jiminy tomorrow, but there's a stack of rooms spare in the house. We're still modifying it, but the staff are going to live at the back when the guests arrive.'

'How many staff are there?' Nat paused and looked up at the waitress as she came back to take their order. 'Two of the house fish and chips, and some bread please. Is that okay, Nell?'

'That's fine. Well, it started with Pippa and Tamsin—Tam is a chef now—and me, of course. We have Evie who looks after the landscaping, and Eliza who is doing the smaller carpentry work when we don't have builders in. She's gone back to Europe for a while but she's hoping to get back before we open.'

Nat raised his eyebrows. 'All women?'

'Well, there's Eliza's . . . friend . . . Phillipe. I think he's coming back, and Pippa was talking about employing him to run the guests over from Hamo and the mainland. He's a very experienced sailor. Oh, and Rafe lives on the island, but he has his own place. He's Pippa's partner.'

'Partner in business or partner in life?'

'In life.' Nell knew she sounded wistful. Would she ever get over this stupid fear of the opposite sex and find a life partner? 'Rafe is Jack Smith, the author. He was living on the island when we arrived.'

'Wow, *the* Jack Smith, the English author?'

'That's him.'

'Sounds like you have an interesting community over there.'

***

Nell's face softened as she looked back at him. He reached across the table and took her hand in his. For a moment his fingers held hers lightly until she tensed and pulled away from him.

'I'm sorry,' he said. 'I just wanted to say thank you for choosing me for the job. I appreciate the work. And I'm looking forward to seeing what's been done over there.'

'As far as I know, you're the only network specialist in the area,' she said.

For a moment Nell's grin was almost cheeky and it reminded Nat of the vibrant woman he had known at university. Seeing how that guy who had assaulted her had taken the life and joy from her personality was hard. If only he'd walked down to the bar with her that night, her life would have been very different.

Nat held her gaze for a while and then he grinned back. 'No, there's a couple up at Bowen and a few in Townsville. But you've picked the best one, Nellie.'

'Such confidence,' she said. 'You haven't changed a bit, Nathaniel Dwyer.'

Nat considered reaching out and taking her hand again, but he hesitated. 'Nell? Can I talk to you some more about what you told me in the car?'

She bit her lip as she stared back at him and nodded slowly. 'What do you want to talk about?' Her tone was defensive, and he was sorry that he'd said anything.

'If there's any way I can help you overcome this. . . this shyness . . . I'd love to help you work through it. You said you didn't go to counselling. How did you cope?'

'I changed my life. I didn't go anywhere except to lectures and I didn't go to any at night. I skipped the night lectures. I took a couple of lessons in self-defence but when the guy asked me why I had decided to do it, I stopped going. I didn't want to talk to anyone. I guess I was so embarrassed about what had happened, I didn't want anyone to know. I blamed myself, and I always felt guilty. I hid behind a confident and mean personality, for quite a while. And that's what you saw that day you came to my office.'

'I can still see the real Nell, you know.'

Her eyes filled with tears as she looked back at him. 'Sometimes I can still feel the old me in there, and then the doubts creep in again.'

Nat put his hands on the side of the chair and gripped it. All he wanted to do was reach out to her.

'I'm a classic case,' she said, bitterness lacing her voice. 'And since all this "me too movement" stuff has been on the news, it's brought it back even more. I did lots of reading back then and I knew the stuff I was doing was a reaction —and still is ten years later.'

'Would it help you to talk about it? You said you never told anyone?'

She nodded. 'Not one person. Not even Pippa and Tam. Oh, don't get me wrong, they knew something was wrong, and they tried, but I didn't spill a word. And you know the best thing?'

Nat swallowed as the first tear spilled onto her cheek. 'What was that?' he asked softly.

'Despite me turning into an utter non-communicative bitch who wouldn't go out with them, they stayed friends with me. Even after Tam moved to the Gold Coast when Pippa and I were at uni, she would ring me two or three times a week, just to talk.'

'I remember what great friends you were.'

'And we still are. They stayed with me through thick and thin, even though they didn't know what was wrong.'

'I'm sure you were a good friend back to them too. It's in your nature, Nell.'

She dug out a tissue and wiped her eyes. 'Sorry. Yes, we've all had our ups and downs, and we were both there for Pippa when she went through a hard time. I guess what I learned from it is that others can carry stuff inside and put on a brave face to the world. Pip was a master at that and then she'd crash and burn. But she's okay now. Her aunt leaving her the island has been amazing for her. For all of us actually. We have a pretty good life.'

'I'm looking forward to seeing it.' Nat said as he wondered whether to let go or push it as Nell had opened up to him.

'Did I ever tell you my Mum was a psychologist?'

Nell shook her head.

'She still has her practice in Brisbane. When I was a kid, I couldn't get away with much. Mum always seemed to know when I'd done the wrong thing. She used to tell me it was written all over my face.' He clenched his fist beside his thighs. 'But Nell, she taught me a lot, and one of the big lessons was about facing your fears. I guess I'd be right in saying that you've never done that?'

'You'd be right.' Her voice was soft. 'I've avoided men, and over the years I've adapted the way I do things to stay safe, rather than facing my fears. Or talking about them.'

'Would you let me help you? I mean, I really appreciate that you trusted me enough to tell me what happened back then.'

She took a deep breath and her shoulders relaxed. Slowly, tentatively her hand reached across the table. Nat lifted his hands onto the table and waited patiently, as Nell's hand crept onto his.

'Would you really do that?' she whispered.

'Yes. Don't you think it's time you re-joined the world?'

She cast her eyes down, and he was worried he'd gone too far. The last thing he wanted to do was push Nell away. Finally, Nell looked up at him and her eyes were bright with hope.

'It's way past time.'

Her hand was still in his when the waitress brought their meals to the table.

Chapter Eleven

Nell woke the next morning to the sound of a trolley being dragged along the path beneath the apartments. At the same time, a boat motor started up and a couple of seagulls swooped past the bedroom window, their squawks raucous. She lay on her back and put a hand over her eyes. It was a change to wake up to all this noise; she had become used to living over on Pentecost Island where the only noise in the morning was usually Tam banging about in the kitchen or Evie heading out to the garden. Occasionally Evie started the mower early, but she soon learned that Nell liked to sleep in after working late into the night.

Talking to Nat last night made her think of the friendships she had. Pippa and Tamsin were always there for her, even when she refused to ask for help. The opportunity that Pippa had given them, to be a part of her venture on Pentecost Island one Nell would always be grateful for.

But she couldn't hide there forever. Maybe a couple of years, until Pip got the place up and running, and then it would be time to go back to the real world and build up a career.

It would be hard to leave. Nell loved living on the island, but she realised she was cocooned in a false sense of safety. Once the guests started to arrive, she was going to have to get used to having other people around and it was time that she did something about her behaviour.

Warmth settled in her chest as she thought back to last night and Nat's offer to help her to adjust. Spilling her story to him seemed to have shifted something inside her and she felt lighter today than she had for a long time.

It was time to make changes in her life. In fact, it was way past time to pull up her big girl panties. She rolled her eyes at the analogy— maybe not a good one – but it was time to put things into perspective and learn to cope with being a little bit more normal. She wondered if Nat realised what a huge thing it had been for her to put her hand in his last night.

But once it was there, she had been able to leave it there. It had felt good

And right.

It wasn't as though Nat was the sort of person who would take advantage of her. She knew that so there had been no fear.

Despite his reputation on campus at university as a "love 'em and leave 'em" ladies' man, he had always been polite and a perfect gentleman to her.

Today when they met, she was going to try to be a tiny bit normal again. Maybe put her hand on his again. Maybe touch his shoulder, or maybe greet him like normal people greeted each other instead of crawling back into her shell. That imaginary shell that had kept her safe for a long time. No one was going to hurt her in broad daylight, least of all a man she had known and trusted before that awful night.

Her breath hitched in her throat as she thought of the effort it would be to do that.

One day at a time, Nell. One day at a time.

She jumped out of bed with new energy in her step and made herself a cup of coffee before wandering out onto the veranda to watch the marina wake up for the day.

The early ferry's horn blared as it came into the marina, and the passengers disembarked. A group of people chattering in a dozen different languages walked along below the apartments looking tanned and happy and carefree. They'd obviously been out on the islands relaxing and having a good time.

That's how Nell wanted to be—well maybe not the tan, she didn't have the skin for that—but to have that lightness and happiness that exuded from those people walking past.

There was no reason why she couldn't do it. But could she really accept Nat's offer to help her?

What would that sort of help look like? What would she have to do?

With a frown she looked across the park that was to the town side of the apartments, as she pondered his offer. She'd leave it for later; there was a beautiful morning out there to enjoy.

Two rows of brightly coloured tents lined the foreshore. She'd heard there were markets on at Airlie Beach a couple of times a week. Quickly finishing her coffee, she headed for the shower.

Fifteen minutes later Nell was wandering along through the markets, looking at the stalls. The tents edged the sand and the gentle whoosh of the small waves was overlaid by the happy chatter of the early crowd. A stall filled with exotic vegetables and herbs beckoned—Tam would love it—and by the time Nell had completed her purchase, she was carrying three large bags.

The next stall sold handmade baskets and she quickly added a basket to her purchases, transferring the produce into the woven basket.

'Planning on lots of cooking, love?' the man asked, and she smiled back.

'Not me.'

Stalls loaded with hats, sunglasses, and an array of clothes lined the foreshore. Nell was tempted by the fragrant aroma coming from the food stalls and wandered over. She bought an egg and bacon roll at one and stood there watching a sand artist create a dragon in the sand.

Her problems with the network, and her worry about the changes she was going to try to make in her life dissolved in the early morning warmth. She chuckled as the artist lit a small fire in a round metal receptacle and put it inside the dragon's mouth.

When she'd finished her breakfast roll, she pulled out her phone and glanced at the time. She had an hour before she was due to meet Nat at the ferry terminal. Two unread messages sat in her inbox, and she realised they must have come in last night when they were at dinner and she had turned her phone to silent.

One from Pippa: **Forgot to tell you. The new girl is Gina. She will meet you at Hamo at noon at Jiminy's boat.**

Nell quickly texted back. **Okay. All good. See you this afternoon.**

The other text was from Tam, and Nell smiled

If you get to the markets on your way back, I would love a new dress. Something stunning to wear to our opening. You should get one too Nell.

Her fingers flew over the keys. **OK, on it. What colour?**

Yellow, with a smiley face and a love heart was the instant reply.

Nell put her basket over her arm and hurried across to the dress stall she had noticed on the way in.

There was a huge selection of styles and colours filling the tent; her attention settled on a bright red and yellow dress that she knew Tam would love. A sweetheart neckline and cinched in at the waist, it was the epitome of the vintage fifties style that Tam loved and carried off so well. Nell pointed to it and the woman behind the table lifted it down.

Nell looked at the label and the price and nodded to the woman. It was Tam's size and she pulled out her purse. 'I'll take it, please.'

'I think it will be a little bit big for you, love,' the woman said. 'It's a fourteen, and you look like an eight to me. Do you want to try it on?'

'Oh no, it's not for me it's for a friend. It's her size.'

'Can I tempt you with something for you?' The woman was obviously a good salesperson. She pointed to a short floral dress hanging on the back wall. 'With your fair skin and your pretty hair, that dark green would look fabulous.'

Nell took a step back and looked at the dress hanging up. 'I don't wear dresses often,' she said hesitantly. 'And especially not that short.'

The last time she'd worn a dress was when Pippa and Tam had made her dress up on Hamo on their way to the island for the first time, and the barman in the Italian restaurant had tried to flirt with her. That had sent her spiralling down for days, but she'd never told them that. Pippa hadn't noticed because she had only had eyes for Rafe that night—it was the first time she had seen him— and Tam had been too busy checking out the menu. It wasn't their fault, and she knew they had only been teasing that night. Tam and Pippa would never do anything to hurt her deliberately.

'What do you think, love?' The woman's voice interrupted her musing and Nell jumped.

'Come on, there's a changing area over here at the back of my tent.'

Nell put the basket down on the grass and took the dress that the woman held out and slipped behind the makeshift change room. She stepped out of her shorts and T-shirt and slipped the silky dress over her head. The fabric was cool and silky against her skin, cooler than shorts and a cotton T-shirt that had hugged her limbs in the early morning tropical heat.

'Got it on yet?'

Nell stepped slowly out from behind the curtain and the woman put her hands on her hips and nodded. 'I'm not just saying it because I want a sale. That dress was made for you. It's stunning.'

Nell chuckled. 'You're a very good saleswoman. But I do love it. It feels great.'

'And, sweetie, it looks fabulous. It's only twenty bucks and I've got it in other colours too.

Something shifted inside Nell and she looked around the tent at the different coloured dresses blowing in the light breeze.

'Yes,' she said slowly. 'I'll take this green one and the red one, the blue one and what do you think about the white one?'

'Hon, with your colour, I'd avoid the white, How about the black. A girl can always do with a little black dress.'

'You're right, and I know exactly the occasion for it.'

The woman was full of questions and Nell told her about the resort and the opening coming up.

'Sounds great. I'll have to get my hubby to bring me out there. We live on our boat. It sounds right up our alley.' She tapped her finger on her chin as she looked down at Nell's joggers. 'You know, I've got a lovely pair of sandals that will match that green dress.'

By the time Nell had paid for the dresses, and three pairs of sandals, and had been talked into keeping the dress and sandals on, the market was getting crowded. She glanced at her watch and gasped, hurrying along the path that led back to the apartments. The black and brown wooden necklace that the woman had placed around her neck as a thank you for her large purchase, moved against her bare skin as she almost ran back to the building. Her shorts and T-shirt and joggers were in a bag on top of the new clothes and the veggies. By the time she stepped into the lift, Nell's hand was chafed from holding the handle of the now heavy basket. She hurried into the apartment, used the bathroom and glanced in the mirror as she washed her face and hands. A stranger with flushed cheeks, and wearing a green dress looked back at her.

Hmm. Different. But okay.

There was no time to change and she grabbed her laptop and bag, juggling them with the basket that now seemed heavier than ever. She left the security card on the kitchen counter, did a final check that she hadn't left anything and pulled the door shut behind her. Luckily it was only a hundred meters across to the ferry terminal, and she made it with minutes to spare.

Chapter Twelve

'It's important that you understand what actions she's taken to protect herself and understand how she feels about that. You will have to be very careful, love. You're not a professional.'

'No, but I am a friend. But, thanks, Mum. I knew you'd be able to give me some advice.' Nat tucked his phone between his shoulder and his ear as he pulled his wallet out to pay for his ticket to Hamilton Island, at the same time keeping an eye out for Nell at the entrance to the terminal. It was close to ten-thirty and the building was milling with tourists, backpackers and workers heading to the island for the midday shifts.

'I know you'll go carefully, darling, but you said it's been ten years. If it's taken her so long to talk about it to anyone as she told you, there will be long-term effects, and you'll have to go very gently if you're to help her. Tell her to make an appointment if you think she'd come and see me. Some professional help wouldn't hurt. Have I met her? Was she ever a girlfriend?'

'No, Mum. Just a uni friend.' Nat chuckled. 'Did you forget I've moved? I'm back up in the islands.' Nat shook his head as he smiled to himself. His mother was very good at what she did, but she could be vague at times.

'Sorry, and yes, of course I do know you moved. It just slipped my mind for a moment. I hate you being so far away, I'll have to come and visit. Well, if your friend is ever down this way, I'm here, or I can give you the name of a good psychologist in Mackay.'

'Okay, if that's needed. I'll call.'

'And like I suggested, the most effective treatment if there are any risk avoidance behaviours, is probably systematic desensitisation. I'll email you some links.'

'Thank, Mum. I've got to go. Love you.'

'Love you too, Nat. You're a good boy.'

Nat chuckled. 'I'm almost thirty-one, Mum.'

'You're still my boy, and you always will be. Check your email.'

'Yes, Mum.' Nat disconnected the call and slipped the phone into his shirt pocket before he paid for his ferry ticket. There was still fifteen minutes before he was due to meet Nell; he checked around but there was still no sign of her. He found two vacant seats together, put the carton of networking equipment on the floor, sat down and opened his laptop. He smiled as Outlook dinged with an email from his mother. Vague, but reliable.

There were confirmation emails from the insurance assessor, and one from the car service place, with a quote for fixing his car.

Nat groaned. Maybe he'd be better off buying another car. He sent a quick email back, asking them to wait a couple of days and he'd been in touch.

The calls Nat had made this morning had achieved what he'd been after. He'd organised for an insurance assessor to come out to the house on Friday and transferred a couple of his non-urgent jobs at Hamo to later in the week. He was free now to give Nell two or three days on their island if the problem was what he thought it was going to be.

First up this morning, he'd called his mate, Brian, at the computer store at Cannonvale.

'I need some gear, mate, and I don't have transport.' Nat listed what he needed. 'I'm over at Port of Airlie and heading out to Hamo. Sorry for the short notice. Add twenty bucks to my bill and put it in a taxi for me.'

'No prob. I'm on it now. I've got all that in stock. Is that all you need?'

Nat frowned. 'I'm not sure what the Wi-Fi is like out there so throw in some ethernet cable and connectors too. Thanks, Brian. Appreciate it.'

Brian had put the equipment Nat had ordered in a taxi and sent it to reception at the apartment, and now Nat was pretty much prepared for any problem he might encounter in Nell's network.

He clicked on his mother's email; in the subject line, he read Physiological and Psychological Desensitisation. He was pleased to see the article was written in layman's terms, rather than the scientific language Mum mostly talked in, and he focused on the content for five minutes before thoughtfully closing the laptop.

Without knowing what he was doing or what it was called, he had actually carried out what the article was talking about with Nell last night when he'd touched her hand.

And she'd responded.

Who needed a psychology degree? Most of it was common sense. Nat grinned wryly; there was no way he'd ever say that in front of his mother.

He glanced at his watch and stood, picking up the box, and his bag before he made his way over to the entrance to the ferry terminal to see if Nell was on her way across. He hadn't known whether to buy a ticket for her; she might have a season ticket with the ferry line. If she was much later, they'd miss the ferry and be late for Jiminy.

A woman in a green dress juggling a basket passed him at the door. He went to step outside and look across to the apartments to see if there was any sign of Nell, when a familiar voice called him.

'Nat!' Nell's voice held amusement. 'I'm here.'

He stopped and turned slowly, and his heart lifted a couple of beats as he looked down at Nell's smiling face.

Nell in a green dress. He had walked straight past her.

Nat stumbled over his words, feeling like a gawky adolescent. 'Oh, um. Sorry, Nell. I . . . didn't see you. I was looking for someone in shorts.'

Not a gorgeous woman in a short dress displaying legs that went forever. Jesus. How could a change of clothes make someone look so different?

Drop dead gorgeous. She took his breath away.

He dropped the carton to the floor and set his laptop on top of it. 'Here let me take some of that off you. Have you got a ticket yet? I didn't know whether to get you one or not.'

'No. I haven't. If you can keep an eye on my stuff, I'll go and get one now.'

'Sure.' He held his hand out for her basket and she set her laptop and bag on top of his.

'I won't be long,' Nell said.

Nat tried not to look after her as Nell hurried across to the counter, but he couldn't help himself. He was finding it hard to reconcile this woman with the one he'd had dinner with last night. Not only was she dressed differently, but her hair was different too. Last night she'd worn it scraped back. Today her hair was loose, falling around her face in soft waves.

Bloody hell. His heart was still pounding. Nat had spent a lot of time with women over the past ten years; he enjoyed their company, and he had several close female friends. He'd even had a couple of relationships that had fizzled out when he hadn't been prepared to commit on a more permanent basis, but he had remained friends with Josie and Ellen.

'It's okay, I'm not heartbroken,' Ellen had said on their last date. 'You'll meet the right partner, one day, Nathaniel. And when you fall, you'll fall big time.'

He hadn't fallen as Ellen had predicted. And never in all that time had one woman brought him to this state. He shook his head trying to figure out what it was that had reduced him to a quivering mess. His heart was still thudding, he was hot and his legs felt shaky.

What the hell was wrong with him? Maybe he had food poisoning?

He took a deep shuddering breath and straightened when Nell walked back over to him, holding her ticket in her hand.

It was just because she looked so different; that's all it was. Nothing more than that; he'd got a surprise when he'd seen her. That's all.

But as he watched her walk over, his breath caught, and a warm feeling settled low in his belly.

And it had nothing to do with the fish he'd eaten last night or the one wine he'd had with dinner.

He was in trouble here.

And in trouble with a woman who was just learning to trust him.

A woman he couldn't afford to hurt.

***

Nell was standing beside Nat on the back deck of the island ferry. A stiff breeze blew from the southeast, and small waves with white foam curling on their tops dotted the Passage across to Hamilton Island as they left the bay. She had decided to stand out on the back deck rather than sitting with most of the passengers in the enclosed air-conditioned cabin; the diesel fumes seemed to filter into the sealed doors. They passed half a dozen yachts with their sales billowing, taking advantage of the strong breeze. A red thunder cat roared past, and Nell caught a glimpse of excited faces as the boat sped past. One day when she was comfortable in her own skin again, she'd love to do that. Take a day off with Tam and Pippa and have some fun, instead of working twenty-four-seven.

Guilt trickled through her. How could she think that when she lived on one of the islands? She was so lucky—they were all lucky—that Pippa had asked them to join her up here. She could still be working in an office at the Gold Coast.

Nat had seemed preoccupied, and she had stayed quiet for the first part of the trip. After all, it was business, and he wouldn't expect conversation. After a while, the silence became a bit uncomfortable and she decided to chat to him.

'It's good outside. Fresh air,' she said leaning over to Nat so he could hear her words over the roar of the diesel motors. 'That smell makes me feel ill sometimes, especially when it's a bit bumpy like today. I'd much rather be out here. Are you happy to be outside too?'

'Yeah. There's a much nicer view out here,' Nat said. 'I can't believe that passengers sit in there watching the scenery on the television when they could be out here seeing the real thing.'

'It's a bit windy out here though,' Nell said, but Nat shook his head and pointed to his ear.

'I can't hear you,' he yelled.

'It's a bit windy out here, I said,' she yelled back, leaning over closer to him. As she moved, Nat had the same idea, and their cheeks brushed against each other.

Nell froze as the warmth of his skin burned against her face. She jumped back, her blush heating her face even more.

Her face burned with embarrassment when the wind caught her dress and lifted it, showing off her black lacy knickers. If there was one thing she had indulged in over the past few years, it was pretty underwear beneath the plain shorts and tees. No one ever saw it and it made her feel a little bit pretty beneath the drab shorts and tees. Nell grabbed at the hem and pressed the fabric against her thighs as she walked across to the railing and leaned against it.

Used to her usual shorts, she'd forgotten what the wind could do to a dress. But to Nat's credit, he looked away, but Nell could see the sides of his lips tilting up as he tried not to smile.

She pulled a face at him and pointed to the door and called out. 'Maybe we should go inside? That wind is getting stronger.'

'If you want to.' This time his grin was wide. 'Like I said I'm quite enjoying the view out here.'

Her face stayed hot as he grinned at her, and finally, she smiled back.

'How about a cold drink or a coffee inside?' Nat walked across to the edge of the deck and stood beside her again.

Nell nodded and pressed her hands to her thighs as they made their way inside. They'd stowed their laptops, her basket and Nat's carton of networking equipment in the luggage bay behind the seats. She glanced over as they went into the cabin to make sure everything was still there.

All good. The basket of vegetables was still on top where she'd left it.

They sat quietly as they drank the coffee that Nat had collected at the bar. The only sound was the low hum of the motors and the quiet conversations of the other passengers.

Nell looked through the salt-stained windows, lost in her own thoughts as they ploughed through the waves on the way to Hamilton Island. It was strange; she was feeling so different today. She'd woken up in a calm and relaxed mood—for a change—and then the saleswoman at the markets had made her feel good when she'd told her how lovely the dress looked.

She allowed herself a sideways glance at Nat, but he was staring ahead, a frown wrinkling his brow.

She hadn't missed his reaction when he'd spotted her in the terminal, and as much as she hated to admit it, she had taken some feminine pleasure from the admiration that had been in his eyes. Maybe that was one step towards healing; she hadn't felt that way for a long time.

But it was probably because it was Nat. She trusted him.

She doubted she would have felt like that if it had been another man.

The trip was quick and within an hour the ferry turned into the quiet waters at the marina at Hamilton Island.

'Right to go?' There was an intense look on his face as he held out his hand to help her up from the low seat. Nell hesitated and reached out and when she took his hand, his smile was sweet. She had forgotten what a good-looking guy he was.

His fingers were firm and cool, and he kept hold of her hand as she stood beside him. A sudden lightness filled her as the tension left her body.

'Nell?'

'Yes?'

'I'd like to take some time with you after I have a look at the network. It's not the right time to talk now, we'll be meeting Jiminy and your new staff member soon. Can we set aside some time tonight to have a talk? I think . . . I'd like to think . . . I can maybe help you. If that's okay with you, that is.'

Nell looked down at their fingers and exhaled quietly. She nodded as she looked back up and saw the worry in his eyes. 'Yes, Nat. We can talk. God knows I've avoided asking for help for a long time.'

He squeezed her hand. 'As long as you know you can trust me. I'd never do anything to hurry you, or make you feel uncomfortable.'

'I know that.'

He dropped her hand and nodded. 'Come on then. We'll get our stuff and go find Jiminy.'

'Better not be late. It's good of him to take us over and save Pippa a trip.'

Chapter Thirteen

'Hey, Jim Boy!' Nat picked up his pace for the last few metres of the wharf. Nell strode along beside him. Jiminy's launch was in the same place as last time and he was at the front of the boat talking to someone on the wharf.

He looked up and waved back. 'Hey, Nat! What are you doing here? I thought you were a landlubber these days.' Nat reached the boat and Jiminy leaned over and shook his free hand 'Hi, Nell. How did you get hooked up with my old mate here? You watch him.'

'I knew Nat in Brisbane.' She flicked a glance at Nat. 'A lifetime ago. He's coming out with us to do some computer work at the resort.'

'Great. We can catch up on the way out. Have you met Gina yet?' Jiminy addressed his question to Nell. She shook her head and turned to the woman who was standing a little way away from the bow.

Nell put down her basket and held out her hand as she looked up at one of the tallest women she had ever seen. 'Hi, Gina. I'm Nell. I work out at Pentecost too, and this is Nat.'

'Gina Gagne. So please call me GG.' Her hand was taken and pumped vigorously. Gina—call me GG— was as strong as she was tall, but it was the unusual accent that surprised Nell the most.

'*Bonjour*. I am so excited about coming to your island. Tam has told me all about it, and it sounds amazing.' She turned to Nat and held out her hand, her smile widened. Her other hand went to her hip and she struck a "come hither" pose.

Nell smiled, and tried to push back the little niggle of something that lodged in her chest. Not jealousy.

No.

'*Bonjour*. My, my, aren't you a fine specimen? I'm very pleased to hear you are another worker on the island. For a moment there, I thought you were a couple.' She wiggled her eyebrows and Nell smothered a giggle.

Nat's face coloured as his hand was gripped and pumped by this larger-than-life woman. Tam was going to love her style; her shorts set was vintage, and her hair was wound into a fifties beehive style on top of her head. Gina's expression was bright and full of interest.

What a fantastic asset she would be to their team. Nell could already see her behind the bar talking to customers in that husky voice.

'Um,' Nat said. 'Well, Nell and I—'

Nell surprised herself as she slid her arm through Nat's interrupting him. 'Nat and I are very good friends. I'm so happy he's coming out to the island too. It's good to meet you, Gina. Tell me where are you from? I can't place that accent?'

'Come on board, guys, and we'll get going.' Jiminy interrupted before Gina answered.

Nat looked down at her arm through his, and Nell slowly pulled it away.

How did I do that? she wondered. *More to the point why did I do that?*

Nat met her gaze and she shrugged and smiled.

Gina followed Nat and Nell onto Jiminy's boat. A strong white-musk perfume wafted across to them and Nell smothered her smile when Nat frowned and turned away wrinkling his nose.

'Sorry,' he mouthed when he realised she'd seen him pull a face. He headed over to the helm to Jiminy, as if to escape the women—or one woman, Nell thought. It was the first time she'd ever seen Nat intimidated by a member of the opposite sex.

She followed Gina to the front of the boat, and they settled themselves in the shade underneath the canvas cover as Nat stood beside Jiminy at the helm.

'So where are you from?' Nell repeated.

'I might look and sound French, but I'm from the good ole US of A,' Gina said as she lifted the straw hat she'd been holding and fanned herself. 'South Louisiana, so I'm used to this damn hot moisture.'

'Tam said you're going to be helping out in the bar.' Nell leaned back against the soft burgundy cushions as Jiminy fired up the engines. She looked across and her face heated when she encountered Nat's steady gaze on her.

'That I am, sweetie, and when it gets busy, I'll do some shifts in the kitchen too. I'm so looking forward to seeing your little ole island. I've heard good things about it.'

'You have? We haven't even officially opened yet.'

'No, I know, but there's a buzz about the resort and bar around the islands. You've had a few drop-ins and they're spreading the word fast. Mighty fast. I was talking to different groups in the bar at the Reef Resort and they said it's a must-visit.'

'Pippa will be pleased to hear that,' Nell said quietly. She was a little bit in awe of this woman.

'So, tell me all about you, darlin'. Where do you fit in?'

'I look after the business side of things.' Nell reached down and held her dress flat as the boat backed out of the berth.

'And Mr Gorgeous over there? How long has he been on the scene? I saw the way he looked at you, sweetie, so don't worry, I won't muscle in.'

Nell opened her mouth to deny what Gina had incorrectly assumed, but for some reason, she hesitated. She waved a hand. 'Oh, Nat and I go back a long way. We were at uni together.'

'Well, you hang onto him, precious. He's a keeper, I can see his aura. Gorgeous gold. Once I get settled, I'll get my cards out and we'll have a reading.'

His aura?

'A reading,' Nell repeated in a weak voice. Who the heck was this woman? Nell began to doubt her first impression. She wasn't too sure how Gina was going to fit in on the island after all. Pippa's reaction was going to be very interesting.

'Yeah, look we could have a quick one now.' Gina delved into her hot pink handbag. 'How long does it take to get to this island?'

'Oh, not long. We won't have time,' Nell said hastily. She pointed as Jiminy took the boat around the eastern shore of Hamilton Island. 'Look, see that peak sticking out of the water over there. That's our island.'

'Well, how damn spectacular is that! I sure am looking forward to living on an island. Have you been away long?'

'No. Only one day. What about you When did you arrive?' Nell asked.

'A couple of weeks ago, but I haven't been out there yet. I've been really hoping to get a job out there.

It was all organised by phone. Tam knows I'm a good worker, but your boss wanted to talk to my bosses down at Surfers Paradise. It's been a while since I worked with Tam. I couldn't believe it when she left the restaurant to go and work in a shopping centre. A jewellery store of all things! She should have been wearing jewels, not selling them. There was something strange back then. She decided to pack up and leave at the end of a shift. Didn't even say goodbye. Next I hear she has moved up here! Did you know her before you came to the island? She was one of the best chefs I've ever worked with, and believe me, *bébé*, I've worked with a few.'

Nell was tired of listening to Gina talk. She obviously didn't expect an answer to the questions she was firing as she spoke, because she barely drew breath before she started again.

'Yep, I've worked bars from New York to Paris, and now I can add Pentecost Island to my list. I didn't know what you had there, so I've bought a whole case of all my cocktail mixing gear. Jiminy nearly died when the boxes arrived at the wharf. Between you and me, sweet pea, I didn't think he was too fussed on taking me out there. Until you turned up, I thought he was going to change his mind, but he's good looking too, just like your man. I wonder if he's married. I checked his hand. Not a ring to be seen.'

Sweet pea! Nell had never been called sweet pea in her life.

She nodded, bemused by this Amazon chatterbox, and unable to get a word in. Relief filled her ten minutes later when Jiminy turned the launch into their bay. How were they going to put up with this constant talk? She was pleased she would be able to disappear into the office.

The translucent blue-green of their bay shone ahead and Nell let out a sigh of satisfaction. Glancing over at Nat she saw the amazed expression on his face. Everyone looked the same when they first came to the island; the vista was beautiful.

It was so good to be home. A lot had happened since she'd left. It seemed as though she'd been gone a week, not only early yesterday.

Pippa and Tam were standing on the wharf, and Nell caught Nat's eye and they shared a smile as Gina called a booming hello across the water.

Life at Pentecost Island was getting interesting.

Chapter Fourteen

'Holy hell, Tam, is that your friend?' I stared at the woman who stepped off Jiminy's boat.

Tam didn't hear me; she'd passed me and was hurrying along to the end of the jetty.

'GG,' she squealed. 'You're here!'

The reunion of my friend and her former co-worker reminded me of that scene from *Mamma Mia* where Meryl Steep caught up with her girl band friends. It was almost as cheesy. There was lots of yelling and dancing around, and hugs were shared.

Gina Gagne was certainly a striking-looking woman. I shrugged as I walked along to the boat. Her references had been really good, and Tam had said she was an excellent worker. As long as she worked hard and fitted in with the rest of us, she'd do.

If she didn't, she would go. I was quite pleased with myself. I was starting to get a bit more business sense—mind you, it was Rafe who had all the good ideas—and I'd hired her on a two-week trial.

Nell came off the boat carrying a basket full of produce and shopping bags. I was pleased to see that she looked less tense. My mouth dropped open as I noticed the guy standing behind her.

He looked like Nathaniel Dwyer, her friend from uni. I knew Nell had had a thing for him back then, but she hadn't mentioned Nat for a long time. Tam noticed him the same time I did, and her greeting confirmed what I'd thought.

'Hey, Nat Dwyer. What are you doing out here?'

I reached the boat as Nell answered. 'Would you believe Nat was the networking guy who was recommended to me? I didn't know until I turned up on his door—at his business.'

There was a flurry of greetings and introductions, including a loud one from our newest staff member as she grabbed my hand.

'*Bonjour*, Pippa, thank you so much for giving me a chance. I promise you; I won't disappoint. I say *laissez les bons temps rouler.*'

I raised my eyebrows and switched my gaze to Tam who grinned back at me. I still had enough high school French to understand Gina.

Let the good times roll. As long as you're a good worker, I thought. I wasn't worried about good times yet.

'Yes,' I said rather tersely. 'We hope our guests certainly do have a good time out here. But we're all going to be busy before then.'

'I've gotta head, Pip. Another job on,' Jiminy called out when the various bags and boxes were offloaded. 'Sarah and I will be here for the bar opening next week. Do you want me to bring some passengers out?'

'Great. I'll look forward to seeing you both. Thanks for bringing my cargo over. I'll let you know about bringing guests out. That could be handy, thanks.'

The water swirled behind the boat as he started the motor and the launch cruised out of the bay.

Nat was loaded up with a couple of bags and a box, and I held my hand out. 'Hi, Nat. It's good to see you. Let me carry one of the bags for you.'

'Thanks, Pippa. You're looking good. The owner of a tropical island, I hear.'

'A long way from our uni days, isn't it?' I replied. 'So you're working up here now?'

'Yep. Business is building. I do a fair bit of work on Hamo and I'd heard about your resort. I didn't have a clue it was you guys until Nell came knocking on my door the other night.'

'Pip?' Nell tugged at my arm as I reached over and took one of Nat's bags. 'Nat might have to stay a night or two to get the network running properly. I said we'd be able to find a bed for him. That's okay, isn't it?'

'Sure. One thing we've got Nat is plenty of room. It might be a bit basic, but we've got lots of spare rooms in the house and the outbuildings. Come on, we'll show you around.'

'Thanks. I'm keen to get started.'

I wondered what was going on between Nat and Nell. She walked close to him and their heads were together as they walked across the beach.

Tam had taken the basket from Nell and was walking ahead of them, chattering away to Gina, who was carrying a large box as well as a suitcase. She'd left another one on the jetty and I heard Nat offer to come back for it.

I walked across the sand behind them all and wondered how the dynamics were going to work.

We were growing fast. When Eliza and Phillipe returned—I'd an email overnight to say that they had sorted things much more quickly than they had expected to and would be back in time for the opening. I still hadn't replied to Eliza's email and would reply tonight when I got Nell to check the bookings. I hadn't been able to access anything since she'd left. I was pleased that Nat was here on site to get it fixed.

Eliza was bringing a friend back with them, and she asked if she could book one of the huts.

'No matter if she can't,' Eliza had written, 'she can stay over at Hamilton Island. I want you to meet Sienna. She's a qualified beautician and therapist and can give you some advice about starting up a spa when you're ready. I hope I'm not being too forward, but I know you've talked about it. If not, she wants to come for a holiday anyway, so all's good.'

I had a lot to organise before our launch next week. For a moment, I felt a bit overwhelmed and a flutter of panic stirred in my chest. I hurried to catch up to the others as we approached the house and I couldn't help my smile when Rafe stepped off the verandah to meet us.

***

Nell

Being back on the island and having Nat here where she lived and worked was strange for Nell, but he was keen to start work. His manner seemed a little distant now that they were on the island, and as they walked from the boat to the house his conversation had been all business.

'That's the bar over there, and that's the first of the huts.' Nell gestured down the path that led to that part of the resort. Evie's plants were blooming, and the path was edged with colour. A delectable aroma drifted from the house; Tam had obviously prepared a special lunch.

But Nat didn't appear to notice any of it. He was talking Wi-Fi, and protocols and asking questions. Nat, the friend, has disappeared and been taken over by the networking guru Nell had gone looking for.

Well, I'd found one so I shouldn't be feeling this disappointment, she thought as Nat stopped and gestured to the house.

'The line of sight to the bar and the huts seems to be uncompromised in any way.'

Nell knew she was a bit snippy when she replied. 'That's worked out very well then because we didn't know to consider anything like that. We're certainly not experts as you'll soon discover, but we all do our best.'

'Oh, I wasn't being critical. Please don't think that.'

'That's fine then. I'll show you where the office is and leave you to it.'

'I'll need you there with me, Nell. If that's all right?' Nat frowned.

Rafe was waiting on the verandah and Nell stopped beside him. 'Nat, this is Rafe. He lives over on the other side of the hill.'

They shook hands, but Nat didn't stay to talk as she walked into the house. He was two steps behind her, and she hadn't expected him to follow right away. She wanted to get out of this stupid dress, put on her usual clothes and pull her hair back.

Nell turned around to apologise to Rafe, but Pippa had already reached him, and he had his arms around her.

'Hi, my lovely. I missed you,' he said.

Nell ignored it and opened the office door and stepped inside.

'Make yourself at home. I'm going to get changed and freshen up. I'll be back in ten minutes. If you want to log in, the admin name and password are taped to the top of the desk.

'Okay, I'll unpack my gear and get started.' Nat's voice was brisk and businesslike, and Nell felt as though they had gone back a few steps.

Where was the kind man who had listened to her last night?

Her thoughts must have been obvious because he put the box on the chair and came straight over to the door where Nell was standing. 'What's going on? Have I upset you somehow, Nell?

She shook her head. 'No. Why would you think that?'

'You're very businesslike all of a sudden.'

Ha, that was the pot calling the kettle black.

'Well, you're on the clock now, Nat. So, it's all business,' Nell said briskly.

'Fair enough, but the clock will go off at five o 'clock and then we'll have that talk I mentioned. Are you still okay with that?'

She shrugged and stepped away. 'If you want.'

Before Nell could get away, Tam appeared in the hall. 'Hey guys, lunch is ready. I've set the big table on the side verandah. Come and eat while it's hot.'

'I'm fine, thanks. I'm here to work, not to socialise.' Nat's tone was polite.

A shimmer of guilt ran through Nell. She knew she was the cause of that.

'Don't be silly, Nat.' Pippa had appeared in time to hear his refusal. 'I insist. Rafe's looking forward to having a chat with you. I think he gets a bit overwhelmed with all the women here sometimes.'

'I certainly do.'

God, everyone was trying to cram into the office. Nell fought the eye-roll that threatened when Gina's husky voice added to the conversation.

'Yeah. Come on, Nat. I want to talk to you too.'

Chapter Fifteen

Lunch was more a social occasion, rather than staff having a meal break together.

Because that's what we all are, thought Nell. It was strange having so many people here with them.

All staff. Well, apart from Rafe, who was Pippa's partner.

The staff now comprised a chef, an accountant, a gardener, a waitperson, a computer contractor and a boss who did the PR. Evie was still outside; apparently, she was too busy to come in and join them.

Lucky her, thought Nell.

Nell sat there quietly pushing her curried chicken from one side of her plate to the other. In the end, she picked up a pappadam and nibbled on that. Her appetite had gone.

'Aw, Nell, what happened to your pretty dress?' Gina had asked when they came out to the veranda. Nell saw Pippa and Tam exchange a glance, but she smiled amicably. 'I'm back at work now so I'm in uniform.'

The conversation was lively, and Gina's effervescent personality had the rest of them—most—in fits of snorting laughter as she recounted stories of some of her more "interesting" experiences around the world. Nell was horrified by some of her stories.

Gina had certainly had an "out there" career and she wasn't backward in talking about it. Nell sat there and thought she must be a prude.

Or maybe I'm just plain boring these days. Maybe she'd led a sheltered life, but the more she heard of Gina's exploits, the less comfortable she felt. Even

Rafe and Nat were looking a bit discomforted as she kept talking.

'One night when I was working in New York, we had this cross-eyed customer, I mean, I knew he was cross-eyed, but—'

To Nell's surprise, Nat pushed his plate away and put up his hand. 'I'm sorry to be rude, everyone, but I have a lot of work to do. Thanks for asking me to lunch, Pippa. And Tam it was a great curry.' He turned to Nell. 'Will you come and help me log in and get started, please, Nell.'

Relief shot through Nell and she nodded. Nat held her chair steady when she stood. 'Thank you,' she said quietly.

It seemed to be the catalyst for everyone else to leave.

'I'll have to make a move too.' Rafe stood and nodded to Tam. 'Thanks for a great meal. I've got a book waiting for me at home.'

Gina chimed in. 'Oh, *daahling* Rafe. Do you like to read? I've always got my li'l ole nose stuck in a book.'

If you ever stopped talking long enough to do that, Nell thought uncharitably.

'Maybe I could come over and borrow one. I'd love to hear what you like to read,' Gina persisted. 'A man who wants to get home to read. How wonderful!'

Pippa stood and she didn't look at all impressed. 'You'll find a considerable amount of reading material in the living room, Gina. Come with me and I'll show you your room in the *staff* quarters.'

It was the first time Nell had heard Pippa talk about the house in that way, and she got the distinct impression that Gina was about to learn her place in the scheme of things. A shame that things were going to change, but she guessed it would be inevitable when the resort was open, and they had more staff here.

All the more reason to get the network up and running.

'Come on, Nat, I'll get you started.' She froze when his warm hand settled gently against her back.

Her indrawn breath must have made Nat realise what he had done, and he quickly moved back, dropping his hand. No one else noticed as there was a lot of movement and talk around the table as Tam and Pippa cleared the plates.

Nell slipped quietly inside and headed for the office, not surprised to hear Nat walking close behind her through the living room.

She could hear the amusement in his voice as he pointed to the bookshelves. 'Pippa was right, you've got a lot of books here.' He crossed the room and stood there looking at the titles. 'A great collection and some classics there too.'

'Most of them belonged to Pip's aunt. The one who left her the house. We found them packed carefully in crates in the back shed. Do you like to read?'

'I do. When I have time. Does that surprise you?'

'No? Why should it?'

'I guess because we don't know each other very well. I'd like to remedy that though, Nell. I missed you at uni after we changed courses.'

'We'll see what happens.' She felt self-conscious when Nat said things like that. When they'd been off the island, it had been easier for some reason. Now she was back in familiar territory, she was extra sensitive. 'At the moment though, our priority is getting this system up and running.'

'It is, come on. Are you happy to sit with me for the first little while in case I have questions?'

Nell nodded. 'I might as well, there's nothing else I can do until you get it up and running.'

The desk holding the main computer wasn't very big and their chairs were close together. Once Nat managed to log in and keep the network up, he reached over and pointed to different things on the screen with each question.

'Is this the icon you use to see if the clients are attached to the network?'

Each time he did, his arm would brush against hers and his thigh pressed against her leg.

She nodded. 'Yes.'

'There's the first part of the problem,' he said.

Nell leaned forward, keen to see what he was looking at but reluctant to move any closer.

'Would it be easier for you if I stood?' he asked kindly.

She shook her head. 'No, that's silly, Stay there. I'm fine.' But her breathing was a bit ragged. It was hard to focus on the screen and listen to Nat's deep voice as his finger traced the network setup on the large screen in front of them.

It took a while, but Nell admitted to herself, that she enjoyed sitting close to him.

'So that's what we have to do, to get this end sorted. It won't be too hard, but it will take the rest of this afternoon and a chunk of tomorrow.'

'If you're happy to come in here with me after dinner tonight, I usually work in here until very late.'

'Uh uh. Not tonight. We have a date, remember.'

'A date? I don't recall that.' She moved away slightly.

What was he playing at?

'Not a date then. A talk. You agreed to set some time aside so we could talk.'

'I'm sorry, with all the fuss and bother here at lunch, I forgot all about that.'

'So, are we on then? I'd like to maybe go for a walk. Somewhere we can talk without interruption. I don't want you to feel uncomfortable, Nell. The reason for this is to make things easier for you. I've got some ideas.'

'It's okay. We agreed.' She tipped her head to the side and shifted her gaze to him, aware that he'd been looking at her for a minute or more. 'I agreed.'

'Excellent.'

Chapter Sixteen

Nell led the way down to the place on the beach where the girls usually watched the sunset and celebrated another day. The same spot where Tam had rescued Eliza when she had arrived on their island.

They were earlier than usual, and although the sun was low in the sky—it was an hour until sunset—and they had no bottle of bubbles or glasses with them.

Pippa and Tam had been curious when Nell had asked them to come down to the beach with her.

'Too early for bubbles? Tam asked.

'Yes, I just want to talk to you both. It won't take long,' Nell replied. She didn't want Gina listening to their conversation. Evie was mowing down around the huts, and Nat was immersed in wires, cables, routers and other bits and pieces that Nell hadn't heard of before.

And Gina—well, who knew what she was doing—she had made herself right at home in a very short time. Nell had already noticed Pippa looking at her with concern in her expression a couple of times.

But before they sorted the Gina situation, Nell wanted to get something off her chest. Now that she had told Nat what had happened at university, she knew that she owed it to the girls to tell them. Maybe that would help her on her journey of healing; maybe she should've done it a long time ago.

There were lots of maybes.

Nell headed over to the flat rock on the north side of the beach.

'Okay, Nell, spill.' Pippa sat on the rock beside her. It was still warm from the sun and Tam sighed as she leaned back.

'Oh, that feels so good. I could go to sleep here.'

'Don't do that. I want to talk to you both.' Nell sat straight as nerves played around in her stomach.

'What's up? I'm worried you're going to tell us one of two things,' Pippa said. 'Had you already decided you want to leave or has Gina brought you to that point in one afternoon? If so, I fully understand, But Nellie, you're not going anywhere.'

Nell couldn't help but laugh. 'No, silly it's neither of those, although Gina is 'a bit of a unit.'

Pippa and Nell looked at Tam. She raised her hands. 'Trust me, gals. GG'll be fine. She's a good worker and she's always been a bit over the top. She's been much worse today because would you believe she doesn't have a lot of confidence?'

Pippa and Nell both shook their heads and spoke together. 'No.'

'Okay, maybe she's changed a little bit since I knew her, but trust me, she's still a great bar person. The customers loved her down at Surfers.'

Pippa looked thoughtful as she stared out over the water. 'She's got almost two weeks to prove herself, including the bar opening, and that worries me a little bit. While Nat's here, we'll go down to the bar tonight, and Rafe can come over, and we'll see how she goes. I'll ask her to tone her performance down a bit. I don't think our sailing clientele will appreciate the over-the-top act. But nothing personal, please, Tam. If she doesn't work out, she'll go after the two weeks. Do you think she'll be okay for the opening?'

'Maybe,' Tam said slowly. 'I would have said certainly before today, but I guess I'm a bit worried too, to be honest.'

Pippa rolled her eyes. 'Okay, tonight will be her main trial. I told her to go down and we'd all come down about seven. Anyway, we didn't come down here to talk about Gina, or GG or whatever her name is. If she's not the problem, what's up, Nell?'

'I need to tell you both something.'

Tam narrowed her eyes. 'Does it have to do with Nat?'

'Not completely, but sort of,' Nell said. 'Nat and I had a bit of a heart-to-heart last night, and it's really helped me, and made me realise that I haven't been honest with you. You're my best friends and because I've told Nat something, I need to tell you. You've been really patient with me. I should have told you a long time ago.'

'Told us what?' Pip said. 'Is there something wrong with you?'

Nell chuckled, but it was from nerves more than mirth. 'No more than usual, but I'm hoping that I'm going to get a bit better over the next few months. Things are going to change. Hopefully.'

Tam reached over and took her hand. 'You're talking in circles, love. What's going on?'

'What's going to change?' Pippa asked with a frown.

'Me. I'm going to try to be more confident and outgoing,' Nell said.

'I thought you looked a little bit more out there than usual when you got off the boat before,' Pippa said.

As usual, she was the one to cut straight to the chase. 'What's caused all this? Nat?'

'In one way,' Nell said.

'You looked gorgeous in the green dress,' Tam said squeezing Nell's fingers. Tam had always been the intuitive one, and she obviously knew this was a hard conversation for Nell to have. 'I haven't had a chance to say thank you for my dress yet. It's absolutely gorgeous. You know me well, sweetie.'

'I had fun at the markets. Would you believe I bought myself more than one dress?'

'Really? No more Nell of the shorts and tees? No way.' Pippa grinned.

'Yep, *and* three pairs of sandals.'

'Has this sudden interest in how you're looking got anything to do with a certain good-looking networking guy?' Tam let go of her hand and looked at her intently.

'Not really, but sort of. In a way, I guess.' Nell stumbled over the words. 'I mean it's not that I'm attracted to Nat—'

Tam raised her eyebrows.

'No, it's not that, at all, Tam. No matter how many faces you pull at me. It's all about me.'

'Oh, for God's; sake, Nellie, stop beating about the bush and tell us. I've got things to do.' Exasperation vied with impatience in Pippa's voice. 'So instead of not really, in a way, you guess, does that mean you're about to run away with Nat? And leave us in the lurch?'

Laughter bubbled up from Nells' chest and it felt good. 'I love you pair, you do know that?'

'Well, tell us!'

Nell looked down at her hands. She wasn't sure how Pippa and Tam would react. Or if the truth be known, she knew them both well enough to have a fair idea. And that's why she was nervous.

'About me having the confidence to dress like a woman again. To have the confidence to be a woman again, and not simply remind myself to be careful with a slash of red lipstick. I've wanted to tell you for a long time. But the more time that passed the harder it was. Maybe I should've told you back then, but I felt so bad about it I couldn't.'

'Back when?' Pippa narrowed her eyes. 'Back at university?'

Nell nodded. 'The night we were supposed to see *Cat Empire*. Actually, the night that you girls did see them.'

'I remember that night,' Tam said. 'We had a fair bit to drink and you decided to go home.'

'I didn't even see the band. I didn't even have a drink.'

'I remember that,' Pippa said. 'I thought it was funny because I knew you were so keen to see them. What happened?'

Nell took a deep breath. 'I decided to walk down from the lecture hall, and I was really excited because Nat said that he was going to come down after he finished a job for a mate. Back in those days we were good friends and that was the first night that I knew that I was interested in him and he seemed different.'

'So, what happened? Did he put the hard word on you?' Pippa said. 'If he let you down, it was because he was a bit of a player back in those days.'

'No! It had nothing to do with Nat. Just let me get to it, will you? I never even saw him again after that lecture. Because . . . because when I was walking back—' Nell's voice broke; even after ten years the memory was enough to make ice run through her veins. She shivered and rubbed her arms.

Tam moved closer and put her arm around Nell's shoulder. 'It's okay, love. Keep going.'

'I took the river path. I was so close to the bar I could see the lights and I could hear the music.'

'What happened?' Pippa's eyes were wide.

'I was assaulted.' Relief flooded through Nell as she finally said the words. They sounded clinical and were detached from the fear that had wracked her body that night. The fear that he was going to hurt her, the fear that her life was in danger.

Her tone was bland. She might as well have said "I went shopping" or "I had dinner."

'Bloody hell.' Tam pulled her into a tight hug and for a moment Nell let her face drop into her friend's shoulder and she shut her eyes.

'Why didn't you tell us, Nell? What aren't you telling us?'

'What sort of assaulted?' Pippa almost growled. 'How bad was it? Did he—'

Nell lifted her head and held Pippa's gaze. 'No. But that was his intent. Someone came along and he put his hand over my mouth. He had a knife. He put it against my throat, and he nicked the skin. I bled.'

Pippa's eyes flashed with anger. 'Why didn't you tell us? Why? I can't understand it. Did you go to the police? Did you tell anybody?'

'No. I went home and got in the shower and scrubbed myself red raw. I felt guilty. I thought it was my fault.'

'Are you serious? I can't believe that you didn't trust us, Nell. I know it hurts, but for fuck's sake, we were supposed to be good friends.' Pippa's glare was unforgiving, and anger rippled through Nell.

Tam dropped her face into her hands. 'And in the middle of all this, I dropped the bombshell that I was moving out.'

'Is that why you didn't want anyone to move into the apartment? You were scared?' Pippa's face was set.

'I've been scared for a long time.'

'And that's why you wore those ridiculous shorts and T-shirts. That's why you weren't ever interested in guys.' Pippa sat there with her arms folded. 'What's the story with the red lipstick?'

'It sounds stupid now, but that was a daily reminder for me. Not to look attractive, not to look as though I was trying to attract a man.'

'You're right. It was stupid.' Pippa shook her head. 'It just looked stupid.'

'Thanks, Pippa.' Nell was feeling stronger. Now that she had finally told them, it was as though the strength that had surfaced when she told Nat began to grow a little more.

'Well, I'm sorry that it happened but I can't for the life of me understand why you didn't trust us enough to talk to us about it. We could have helped you and taken you to see the right people.' Pippa sat rigidly and stared at Nell.

Nell stared back. Pippa's cheeks were flushed, and her eyes were full of something. Anger?

Disappointment? It was hard to tell. 'I blamed myself. I told you I didn't want *anyone* to know.'

'How could you possibly blame yourself? God, how stupid could you be?'

Nell's mouth dropped open. This was not how she had expected the conversation to go. 'Stupid? You're calling me stupid? Thanks for the support, Pippa. I've been calling myself stupid for the past ten years.'

'Pippa, calm down.' Tam's tone held a warning.

'No, I won't. We have a really strong friendship. Or I thought we did. I mean, look how you girls supported me when I was going through all my shit and you really helped me, and I thought we were tight. But then something happens to Nell here, and she shuts herself down and then turns into a person we didn't even like very much sometimes.'

Tam interrupted. 'Hey, speak for yourself, Pippa, and don't be so bloody unsympathetic.'

'No, Tam, you listen too. It really pisses me off that there was no trust there. I don't know if I even know you, Nell.'

Shock filled Nell. 'Hey, I'm the one it happened to. I'm the one who had my life screwed up.'

'And hey, we were friends and we could've been there for you to help you. You should've gone to the police. You should've told somebody instead of having a shower and trying to pretend it didn't happen and look at what it's done to you. You've lost ten freaking years of your life now. I can't believe it. You don't think it was a stupid reaction?'

'No, I don't. Not now.' Nell's words cut the air like a knife. 'I'm sorry I told you. But I've finally admitted to myself it's time for a change. Nat's going to help me.'

'Ah, we couldn't help you, but cute little Nattie can.'

'For God's sake, Pippa. Will you listen to yourself? Stop being such a bitch.' Tam jumped off the rock and stood in front of Pippa.

'Well, she couldn't trust us. How many times over those years have we asked her if something was wrong?'

'Don't talk as though I'm not here! I didn't want to talk about it, and it was my business.' Nell stood up next to Tam, and it was as though they were a united front against Pippa's anger.

'You really think so?'

'Pip, let it go. You are being a total bitch.'

'Well, I'm finding a lot out today. I've had enough and for the record, Tam, I don't like your friend GG at all.' Pippa pushed herself up and headed up the beach.

Nell's eyes filled with tears as she watched Pippa walk away. When she got to the path Nell was pleased when Pippa turned towards Rafe's house.

'Are you okay, sweetie?' Tam put her arm around Nell's shoulder.

'Yeah, I'm fine. I just thought seeing I'd told Nat that it was time I told you and Pippa.'

'At least she can vent to Rafe,' Tam said. 'He's so sensible and calm, he'll calm her down a bit.'

Nell lifted a shaking hand to her mouth. 'I can't believe her reaction. It was as though something happened to her, not me.'

'She'll come around, Nell. You know what she can be like. She still carries a lot of baggage that she keeps hidden.'

'I guess I do know that, but we haven't seen that side of Pippa since we've been here.'

'I can sort of see where she's coming from, but I don't blame you in any way. I wish you told us at the time, but I can truly understand why you didn't. It's one of the worst things that can happen to a woman and I don't know how I would've reacted. But hey, the bottom line is you're here. And hopefully, after all this time you can start to put it behind you. You've expressed that you want to do that, and you will. We're safe here on the island. Pippa will get over her little dummy spit, and you're just going to get better.' Tam kept hold of Nell's hand as they walked back up to the house. 'You feeling okay now?'

'I am.'

Tam glanced at her with a smile. 'You know you looked gorgeous in that dress, don't you? You should have seen the way Nat was looking at you.'

'No.' Nell shook her head and chuckled. 'He looked the same way at Gina—sorry, *GG*—when he saw her the first time.'

Tam's laugh rang out. 'I doubt that very much. It would have been more that he couldn't believe what he was seeing. God, Nellie. I think I've made a big mistake there.'

'I have a feeling you have too. Time will tell,' Nell said with a giggle.

Chapter Seventeen

Pippa

The darkness was deepening as the sun disappeared behind the mountains on the mainland; the rising moon bathed the calm waters of the passage in a cold silver. I tore along the track and up the hill to Rafe's house as fast as I could. My eyes stung, and my throat ached as I fought back tears. All I wanted was Rafe's arms around me, to lose myself in his embrace and feel needed . . . and loved.

There! I'd finally admitted it to myself. Even though he hadn't put it into words, I knew Rafe loved me.

I trembled as a shiver ran down my back when I pushed open the front door. There was no knocking anymore; this was more home to me than Aunty Vi's. What is it they say? Home is where the heart is. Well, my heart was certainly here.

The house was in darkness, but the glow of the lamp on Rafe's desk in his study shone through into the large living room. He was still working, and I hesitated before I stepped into his inner sanctum. Biting my lip, I brushed my hand across my eyes to wipe away the couple of tears that had leaked out despite my best efforts.

Taking a deep breath, I walked over to the desk, and my man reached for my hand without taking his eyes from the screen.

'Just give me about half a minute, love. I've only got one page left to check.' His other finger ran down the large screen and his lips moved as he read the words silently.

I stood, with my hand in his, and stared through the huge window in front of Rafe's desk. In the far distance the mountains were bathed in a soft mauve that transformed into a deep purple and then deepened to black as I waited.

Calm stole through me and my breathing evened out and then the first wave of guilt trickled in. I closed my eyes and focused on breathing evenly, even as panic threatened to overtake me.

What had I done? How much had I hurt Nell?

Tam was right. I had been an utter bitch, but I hadn't been able to help myself.

I jumped as Rafe tugged at my hand, and I was soon sitting on his lap secure in the warmth of his arms.

'Tell me what's wrong,' he said smoothing my hair back from my brow.

'I just needed a hug.'

'I saw you running up the path. You looked like you had the hounds of hell after you. What's happened? I can feel the tension in your body.' His hand reached up and kneaded the muscles at the base of my neck.

'Thank you. That feels good.' I sat straight and rubbed my forehead with one hand. 'I did something awful.'

'I can't believe that.' Rafe pressed his lips to my cheek. 'Do you want to talk about it?'

'I don't know. I don't want you to know what I'm really like.'

His chuckle was low and husky. 'Sweetheart, I think I know what you're like.'

'I don't want you to think less of me. To stop liking me.' A tear plopped onto my hand.

'If you don't know by now that I more than "like" you, you're not very good at reading me. I've never put it into words, because I didn't want to scare you away. What we've got together is much more than "like".'

Rafe lifted his hand and used his thumb to gently wipe away the next tear. 'Pippa, I love you. Maybe it's not the best time to be telling you when you're upset about something, but I don't want you to have any doubts about that. Nothing you could do, or anything you tell me will change that. You are in my soul. And sweetheart, I am not letting go of you; I just hope you recognise what we share.'

My breath hitched as he held my gaze and I was lost in his brilliant blue eyes. I swallowed, determined to let those words out. 'I love you too, Rafe.'

His lips slid slowly down my cheek to my mouth and I closed my eyes, lost in his kiss.

When he finally pulled back, Rafe rested his forehead against mine. 'Well, now that we've got that out of the way, tell me what's upset you so much. But not here at my desk.'

I climbed off his lap and he stood.

'It's a beautiful night. I'll pour us a drink and we'll go and sit outside.'

I followed him to the kitchen and looked around. It was spotless and there was no sign that he had been in the kitchen since he'd come home. I'd tidied the breakfast dishes away before I'd left this morning.

'Have you eaten since lunch?' I said. 'Or even had a coffee? Or a glass of water?'

As Rafe looked at me blankly, his stomach gave a large gurgle.

'I guess that's a no?' I said.

'I wanted to get the book finished.' His smile was wide. 'I'll email the manuscript to Jenny tonight. And besides after that huge lunch, I wasn't hungry.' His eyes widened and he stared at me. 'I know what's wrong! That new woman's upset you! I knew it wouldn't take long. She's a bit of a dill. What's she done?'

I pointed to the fridge. 'You get us a drink, and I'll get some cheese and crackers and then I'll tell you what *I* did. And no, it wasn't Gina or GG, or whatever she calls herself.' I was trying to focus on the mundane—the drinks, the cheese and crackers; the words of love that we had exchanged so unexpectedly had filled me with a warm glow, but I needed to tell Rafe what I'd done before I basked in that feeling.

First, I needed to figure out how to make things better with Nell. How to make her understand why I reacted like that? My stomach clenched as I remembered my cruel words

Soon we were sitting out on the terrace. Small creatures scurried around in the gardens that spilled down the hill—Evie had been doing work for Rafe in her spare time—and the occasional bird called to its mate from the beach below.

Rafe half-filled my wine glass before doing the same to his, and I pushed the plate of cheese across to him.

He chose a sliver of brie and placed it on the cracker before he leaned back in his chair. 'Are you feeling a bit calmer now? Ready to talk?' His eyes were shadowed by the candles I had lit on the table.

'I was horrible to Nell. I really upset her, and I think I've done our friendship some awful damage.'

'Tell me what happened.' His voice was low and soothing. 'And I doubt it. You three are rock solid. I've seen the way you watch out for each other.'

'And I've broken that trust.' I ran my fingers slowly around the top of the glass. 'Nell wanted to see Tam and I. To talk to us. We went down to the beach, and she told us something that had happened to her a long time ago. I won't tell you what it was, because it's not my story to tell, but it explained a lot about the way that Nell is.'

Rafe nodded. 'Nell isn't comfortable around men. I noticed that early on and I've gradually gained her trust, I think.'

'You have. She thinks the world of you.'

'So, what happened then?'

'I was awful to her. I yelled at her, and I made it all about me. I took it personally; the fact that she hadn't told us when it happened.'

'Why do you think you did that?'

'Because she was just one more person who didn't need me. Another one in the long line of people who thought I didn't matter enough.'

'Whoa, slow down there. Nell and Tam love you like a sister. Your friendship is pretty special. You each know what the other is thinking, and as I said, you look out for each other. I doubt very much that you've destroyed that with one argument.'

'It wasn't an argument. It was all me. Nell didn't flare up.'

'Fill me in on this "long line of people" who don't need you.'

I picked up my glass and sipped so I didn't have to answer straight away. 'I guess I was exaggerating. It's only two people. Mainly.'

'Two?'

'You know all about Aunty Vi and how she left me the island.'

'I do,' he said with a chuckle. 'You were the woman who arrived out of the blue. The one I didn't want interfering with my solitude.'

'Until I got stuck up in a tree and you saved me.' I reached for his hand and kept hold of it. 'I haven't told you anything much about my parents, have I?'

'I just know they both passed away and you don't have any siblings.'

'That's right. How my mother died has caused me a lot of grief over the years. You need to know this Rafe, if you want to stay with me. My mental health has always been fragile. The psychologists have always told me it was because of what happened, and not because I've inherited my mother's instability.'

Rafe squeezed my fingers but didn't say anything.

I stared out over the dark sea. It was still hard to talk about, no matter how many therapy sessions I'd sat through over the years. 'I've never shared this with anyone except Nell and Tamsin, and of course Aunty Vi knew. My parents adored each other, to the exclusion of all else, even me. I do think my Dad loved me though. I can remember him holding me, and I can remember his rough cheeks and his special smell. I don't ever remember feeling loved like that by my mother. The counsellor Aunty Vi sent me to when I was in my teens told me I craved love and didn't want to risk losing it. He was talking about Mum, but I know the pattern continued with some of the relationships I've had. I never chose well; it wasn't ever about picking the right person. It was all about wanting someone to love me. To need me. I turned to look at Rafe and his eyes were fixed on me.

'But when I fell for you, it was so different. I fought what I was feeling. I've never fought going into a relationship before. I've always chosen what I wanted to do and been in control. With you, it was totally different; it wasn't me choosing someone I thought I wanted to love or be with. Or someone I wanted to love me. I didn't think I even liked you, but I still remember that first incredible moment when I saw you in that restaurant. I fell in love before I even knew you.'

'And I, with you,' he said softly.

'Sorry, I'm getting off the track here.'

'I like this track,' Rafe said softly, running his thumb over the back of my hand. I'm listening, sweetheart. Go on.'

'I was almost eleven when Dad was killed in a work accident.' I pushed back that ever-present grief and held Rafe's gaze steadily. 'My mum couldn't live without him and she took her own life the same year. That's how I ended up living with Aunty Vi, and that's how I ended up in therapy. And that's why I've always had a thing about being needed by somebody, although I've made some pretty awful choices over the years.' Her voice trembled. 'Nell and Tam have been my rocks, and that's why I was so awful to Nell. My reaction was over the top, but I couldn't help myself. She suffered something dreadful, and all I could do when she finally told us both, was abuse her for not telling us. I am a selfish bitch.'

Rafe let go of my hand and stood. He moved across to my chair and his hands pulled me up into his embrace.

I buried my face in his soft shirt. 'Thank you. I love you so much, Rafe. It's such a relief to be able to say those words and not be judged.'

'We were meant to be together, Pippa. I was destined to come here to this island, and I was here waiting for you to arrive. I think Vi had a hand in it from up there too, don't you?'

'Maybe. I do know she loved me, even though she could be a tough old stick.'

He chuckled. 'That she was. Now, you know there are two things you have to do.'

I pulled away and nodded. 'I know. I have to go and find Nell and tell her how sorry I am.'

'You do.'

'What's the second?' I frowned.

The moon had risen high while we had been talking, and Rafe led me over to a patch of bright moonlight at the edge of the terrace. For the rest of my life, I would remember this moment in the soft white light with the strong spicy smell coming from the tropical creeper that grew along the low trellis.

'I want you to wait here while I get something. Promise me you won't move.'

'I promise.' Curiosity filled me as Rafe hurried back inside.

He was soon back, and he took my hands again. 'I've waited for the right time to ask you, and this is it. I know you're unsettled because of what happened with Nell, so we don't have to tell anyone until you're ready.'

'Ask me?' A strange and unfamiliar feeling ran through my limbs and I trembled. 'Ask me what? And tell anyone what?'

'Patience, sweetheart.' For a long moment, he held my eyes with his, and all the love that I knew he had for me shone brighter than the moonlight pouring down on us.

My mouth dropped open when Rafe dropped to one knee.

'Phillipa Carmichael, will you do me the honour of pledging your life to mine? Will you share your life and your love with me . . . as my wife?' Rafe reached into his shirt pocket and pulled out a small velvet case. 'Not only do I love you, I *need* you in my life to make me whole.

He opened the case and moonlight hit the ring nestled in the white satin casing. Shards of blue and pink light came from a large white moonstone, that was nested in a circle of diamonds.

'I will,' I said simply, never surer of anything before in my life. I held my hand out and Rafe stood and slipped the ring onto my finger.

He pulled me close against his warm body, and the moon shone down on us as I lifted my lips to meet those of the man I loved with my heart and soul.

Chapter Eighteen

Nell

Tam was banging about in the kitchen when Nell went looking for her.

'I don't know if we're going to be down at the bar tonight. Pippa hasn't come back yet, has she?'

Tam shook her head. 'No, not since she went up to Rafe's, but Gina's down there setting up all her cocktail shakers and things ready for the night. She's raided my fridge and taken most of the cream I had, and all my pineapple. I'll get sorted here and have a quick shower and grab Evie. I'll meet you down there.'

'Don't rush. I'll be a while yet. Nat and I are going for a bit of a walk.'

Tam looked at her curiously. 'And you're okay with that?'

'I am. I trust Nat. He wants to help me.' Nell gave a shrug. 'At least I can give it a go.'

'As long as you're comfortable with him.'

'I am. We won't be long, just a bit of a stroll and a chat. We'll come back to the bar. Do you think Pippa will come back?'

'Of course, she will. She'll be over to say sorry to you and—'

'You think?'

'I know. She'll be back because it was her idea to give GG a trial run tonight. She said she'd told her to be at the bar at seven. GG was pretty pumped when she left here.'

Nell wrinkled her nose. 'Pumped about serving drinks to just us?'

'And Nat. And Rafe. I think she might be a bit of a good-time girl. I do remember her down at the coast a few times. I'd forgotten about those nights until I saw her in action. But like I told Pip, she was a good worker and a great person behind the bar. The customers loved her.'

'I wonder if that's the sort of clientele we'll have here though. She didn't shut up once in Jiminy's boat today. She wanted to read my cards!'

'Yeah, she tried that with me too, but I said a polite thank you, but no.'

Nell giggled. 'Might be an interesting night tonight. If Pip's over her dummy spit.'

'She'll be feeling bad, I can guarantee that. You're okay now?'

'Yeah, I've spent the afternoon with Nat, doing what I love best.'

'Oh yeah?' Tam wiggled her eyebrows. 'And what would that be.'

Nell pursed her lips. 'Playing with spreadsheets on the network. Nat's got into the cloud and got all my data back. The accommodation bookings and all your menus and orders.'

'Oh, I love him already.'

'There's still some problems though. It won't stay connected, and he's working on fixing that. He thinks it might take a couple of days.'

'And how do you feel about that?'

'I'm fine. I enjoy his company, and he's taught me a lot about our setup already. By the time he goes back, I should be right, but he's offered to do a fairly reasonable deal, where he can log in remotely if I have any problems. I need to talk to Pippa about contracting him. Once we grow, we're going to have to expand the network.'

'He lives over on the mainland?'

'Yeah, that's another story. In that storm last night, there was a lot of damage to his house. A tree came down and I ended up under the kitchen table.'

'Jeez, you've had a big couple of days, girl. You really are okay?'

Nell nodded firmly. 'I am.' And she meant it. She was feeling good, even after Pippa's rant. Telling Nat, and then telling the girls about the event in her past had lightened the load and she was finally starting to believe that she could return to some sort of normality. Slowly, but surely.

Her face split into a wide smile. 'I'm happier than I have been for a long time. I feel like I've got myself back, if that makes sense.'

'It's good to have you back. Can I ask you one favour though?'

Nell frowned and looked at her friend.

 What sort of favour?'

'I'm going to need a whole heap of cleaning rags?'

'And?'

'A good start would be those awful T-shirts and shorts of yours. And when you go for your walk and come down to the bar, wear one of your new dresses. Start like you plan to continue.'

'Yes, Mum.'

***

Nell slipped into her room and crossed to the small space where she hung her clothes. The house— especially the rooms that the girls had taken for their own—still needed a lot of work. The hanging space was simply a small alcove with a rusted curtain rod jammed diagonally in the corner between two walls. Not that Nell had a lot of clothes to hang. Apart from the new dresses, there were only three others that she'd brought with her when they'd moved to the island. On the other hangers were six khaki T-shirts neatly pressed.

She stood there for a moment before she reached for a short floral dress that she'd fallen in love with at a store in Brisbane years ago, and of course, had never worn. She kicked off her shorts and her T-shirt and pulled it over her head. The tag caught on her ponytail and her hair fell around her face. She grabbed her hairbrush and pulled it through the tangles, and then fluffed it up a bit.

The new Nell. Taking notice of her appearance. She wasn't making the effort for Nat; it was to look presentable in the bar later. She opened her small makeup bag and dug around and pulled out a pale pink lip gloss and smudged her lips. It had been in there so long, it was a wonder it wasn't hard.

A nervous frisson ran through her nerve endings as she slipped on a pair of sandals. They could just go down to the beach, and sit on a rock, and then once they were done talking, they could go over to the bar and see what was happening there.

She composed herself and headed back to the office.

Nat looked up and for a moment his eyes widened as his gaze ran over her, and then his expression cleared.

Oh God, why did I get changed?

'Ready to go for a walk?' he asked.

'Yes, and then we're going over to the bar for a couple of hours. GG's trial run.'

'Okay, wait on the veranda for me. I'll just change my T-shirt and have a wash. I've spent the last half hour on the floor sorting out some cables.'

'Thank you, Nat. I really appreciate what you're doing for us.'

And me, she added quietly to herself.

Nell waited on the veranda. She looked up at Rafe's house on the hill above the bay, but strangely it was in darkness apart from the moonlight shining on the windows that faced the sea.

Maybe Rafe and Pippa were in the bar already?

Nat was as fast as he said he'd be and was back with her after only a few minutes.

'I'm sorry,' Nell said. 'We haven't sorted a room for you yet, have we?'

'No matter. I can bunk down on the sofa in the office if that's okay. '

'No, we'll get a room for you. Eliza's room is made up.'

'Eliza?' he asked. 'I haven't met her yet.'

'Eliza and Phillipe—her friend—have gone to Europe to sort out some stuff, but they'll be back soon. Eliza is a carpenter; she does a lot of the building work here. I think Pippa has some work in mind for Phillipe too—if he comes back with her.'

'You certainly are an interesting group,' Nat commented as they went down the steps. 'Lots of skills between you all. And the place looks great. How long did you say until you open?'

Nell gestured to the path that led to the beach. 'Come this way. I've only got sandals on. The bar opens

Saturday week, and the accommodation is booked for the first few huts the week after that. The bar will have some restaurant service to start with tapas and that sort of thing, but once Eliza's back, she's going to oversee the major renovation of the house. The front living room is going to be a restaurant that leads out to the veranda, and the kitchen will be converted to a commercial standard.'

'Wow. It is going to be a big concern. It sounds great. It's all Pippa's idea?'

'Yes, it's her baby. Financially, it's hers, but we've all been involved in the planning, and yes, it's coming together well.'

'You're going to need a lot more staff.' Nat stood back as the path ended. Nell bent down and slipped her sandals off and left them on a log at the end of the path.

'We are, and I think that's one thing we've been a bit slack on. We've been so busy getting everything done, I think we should have spent more time thinking about hiring staff with suitable skills, and staff who will really fit in with our vision.'

Nat chuckled as they walked along the beach towards the rocks at the northern end. There was just enough moonlight to see where they were going. 'Are you thinking of GG when you refer to fit in?'

Nell sighed. 'Yes, I wonder, but maybe we're judging too quickly. We really need to get our vision statement into a staff manual and be explicit with our expectations.'

Nat stopped and turned to face her. He pointed to her hand. 'May I?'

Nell nodded and Nat's fingers were warm against hers, as he took her hand in his. 'Pippa is really lucky to have you on board. You've had enough business experience to know what needs to be done.'

'Yes, between the three of us, we've covered most bases, I think. We've been lucky with Evie and Eliza. Evie was a uni friend, and Eliza literally washed up in the bay.'

'Really? I'd love to hear that story, but Nell?' His fingers squeezed hers and she looked down at their joined hands. Funnily enough, it didn't bother her; in fact, it was rather pleasant having Nat hold her hand. She looked up at him and stepped back a fraction as his eyes were intent on hers.

His face was all angles and shadows, and her heartbeat picked up as a small trickle of memory ran into her consciousness. She must have tensed because Nat let go of her hand.

'Yes?' she said.

'We're here to talk about you tonight. Come and sit over on that flat rock with me.' His voice was calm.

Nell smiled. 'That's our thinking and drinking rock. There's been a lot of decisions made there.'

'Well, it sounds like a good place to talk. Good vibes.'

Nell climbed up onto the rock. Even though the sun had been gone an hour, it was still warm against her bare legs. The sounds she loved and that were becoming very familiar to her filled the air, the swish of the tiny waves on the shingly sand, the mournful calls of the curlews and the chirping of cicadas in the bush up the hill.

'It's heaven, isn't it,' she said softly as Nat sat beside her.

'Paradise. I don't think I'll ever go back to the city, much to my mother's disappointment.'

'Did you get the insurance sorted on your house this morning?'

'I did, but I'm going to have to find somewhere else to live and maybe an office space to set up my equipment. I was thinking about Hamo, but I imagine the rent there would be beyond me. Anyway, Nell, we're here to talk about you.'

She nodded without speaking.

'I didn't breach your confidentiality—you don't know how much I appreciated that you trusted me enough to tell me what happened at uni—but I spoke to my mother and I've done some reading.'

'Your mother?' Nell didn't know how she felt about that. All of a sudden it seemed a lot of people were knowing what happened. Nat, the girls, his mother—

''It's okay. I told her it was someone I knew but I didn't say where from or how long ago. My mother is a psychologist, and very highly regarded in her field.' He lowered his voice a little. 'She has had a lot of sexual assault clients.'

'Oh.' Nell bit her lip. It was the first time Nat had used those words in relation to "it", and she felt unsettled.

'It's okay, Nell. She sent me a couple of articles and a couple of websites. I'm sure you've read them all, and you know what they say. The thing is reading them, and knowing what to do to get yourself better, is much easier than putting that stuff into practice.'

'What stuff?' she said suspiciously, moving a fraction further away from Nat.

'Have you read about physiological and psychological desensitisation?'

'No.' Nell stared at him. 'I didn't read anything. Then or now. I didn't talk to anyone; I didn't see anyone, and I didn't go Googling anything. I knew how I felt. I didn't need anyone to tell me that.' Belligerence had crept into her tone.

Nat was quiet for a moment, and then his voice was gentle as he replied. 'I'm certainly no expert, but I did a lot of reading about it from the stuff Mum sent to me. You've taken the first massive step by talking about it. Now it's time to put some new habits in place.'

'What sort of habits? What's this desensitisation stuff.'

'Jeez, Nell. I'm going to sound like a psychologist here. Just bear with me. Please? Trust me?'

She nodded.

'It's about confronting your fears. Facing those things and doing the things that you haven't done over the past ten years because you were scared of what would happen, or because you were scared it would bring the fear of that night back.'

'I get that.'

'So, tell me the sorts of things you did to stay safe, and kept you feeling okay about yourself.'

Bitterness surfaced and Nell took a deep breath. 'I haven't felt okay about myself since then.' She stared past Nat over to the water. A boat was slowly making its way down the passage and music drifted across the water. 'To keep myself safe, I wore clothes that would let me blend into the background. I didn't interact with men unless it was necessary in the workplace. I didn't go out after dark.'

'You've come a long way in the last few days. Since you told me what happened. Look at yourself now, Nell.'

'And Tam and Pippa too. I told them this afternoon.'

'Excellent. But look at yourself tonight.'

'How do you mean?'

'By letting it out, you've changed some things already.' Nat gestured to the sky. 'It's dark, and you're out. I'm a man, and you're out here with me. And you're not wearing clothes that would make you blend into the background as you said. You're wearing a colourful dress. In my mother's words, you have already engaged in some psychological desensitisation. And it's been your choice. How are you feeling tonight? Are you scared?'

'Of course not. I trust you.'

She could just see the narrowing of his eyes in the faint moonlight. 'That's interesting because you don't really know me. It's been at least eight years since we last met.'

'But I knew you then, and I guess I'm taking you on trust now.'

'Okay, that's fair enough. What we need to teach you to do is to take people—particularly men—on some level of trust when you first meet them.'

'How is that going to happen?'

'I'm not saying that you can go out and put yourself in dangerous situations. I mean, any woman should be careful about that.'

Nell nodded slowly. Nat was making sense. To overcome her fear, she had to listen to him. 'Yes, I put myself in a foolish situation when I chose to walk through the bush that night.'

'Yes, in an ideal world you could do that, and it's sad that you couldn't. But it comes down to common sense. But we'll talk about that more later. I'm only going to be here for another day or two and I'd like to get to work.'

'Work? What do you mean?'

'I want to help you with the physical desensitisation, Nell.'

Nell ignored the panic that began to rise in her throat. 'Like what?'

'First up, will you read the articles? I want you to understand that the sorts of things I'm going to suggest are based on scientific study.'

Suspicion flared. Was this the Nat of old, just looking for a woman? Was she being completely gullible here? 'What sorts of things?

'A personal question. Have you had any partners since it happened?'

Nell shook her head and her cheeks heated as he continued.

'So, no sexual partners? No sex life?'

'No.' She cleared her throat. 'So, what I'm understanding here . . . that this is all about having sex with you—otherwise couched in the fancy term of "physical desensitisation" and I'll magically be cured.' She swung her legs off the rock and tensed as Nat reached for her arm. 'No, thank you.' Anger flared through her, but no fear. Just anger and a crushing disappointment.

'Stop, Nell. Of course not. That's not what I was talking about at all.' She turned to look at him and he ran his hand through his hair. 'I didn't express that well.'

'What did you mean then?'

'Small steps. Like tonight, you're out in the dark with me. You've let me hold your hand. I meant things like that. God, I'm sorry. I didn't mean it to sound like that at all. You make me sound like an absolute sleaze.' His laugh was bitter. 'I guess I had that reputation back at uni, but there is a story behind that.'

She folded her arms.

'It's things like being comfortable when you stand near someone. Being able to be touched. Platonically! Not flinching if I took your elbow to guide you. Understanding that a simple touch is not physical assault. Look, I'm sorry. I totally stuffed that up. That's why I am a computer bod, and not a psychologist. I'll give you the articles to read before I go. I'm really sorry you thought I was putting the hard word on you.'

He jumped off the rock and stood next to her. Nell reached out and put her hand on his arm and Nat looked down at it before he lifted his gaze to meet hers.

'No, Nat. *I'm* sorry. You've given me absolutely no reason to think that and I shouldn't have reacted so badly.' Surprise flooded through Nell as her fingers tingled to life. Alive from the feel of his skin beneath them. The surprise deepened when she realised that she liked touching Nat and that if she was honest, she was attracted to him.

Just like she had been all those years ago.

Chapter Nineteen

'Nell!' They turned as one when Pippa called from the path. Nell hadn't heard them approaching; she was too immersed in her thoughts and the revelation that had just hit her.

'Excuse me a moment,' she said quietly to Nat. 'I'll just talk to Pippa for a minute if you want to go with Rafe. We have some unfinished business.'

Pippa stepped onto the sand and Rafe waited on the path. Nat did as Nell asked and she stood and waited at the rock for Pippa to come over. The two guys walked up towards the bar together and Nell squared her shoulders as Pippa walked across to her.

'Nellie? I'm so, so sorry.' Pippa held her arms open, but Nell stood there with her arms folded.

Seems like everyone was sorry about things they'd said tonight. Nell surprised herself again. For the first time in a long time, she was strong inside. She'd had the courage to stand up to Nat when she misunderstood his intentions, and now she fronted up to Pippa.

'It's going to take more than a sorry.'

'I know. I was way, way out of line.'

'You were.'

'I can explain, I just want you to accept my apology. I was a cow to you. You dumped something pretty bad on us and I didn't think of you at all. It was all about me, and my 'woe is me' nobody loves Pippa.'

'It was.' Nell's arms were still folded. A glimmer of sympathy rose in her chest, but she was not going to give in easily. 'Did Rafe make you see sense?'

'No. I knew how awful I'd been before I even got there.' Pippa's mouth lifted in a small smile. 'But yeah, Rafe told me I had to come and apologise before I did anything else.'

Nell nodded.

'He also told me how stupid I was to compromise the friendship we have. He told me how special it is. I know that, Nell. And I know I put it at risk by only thinking about me.'

'You did.'

'So?' Pippa's voice shook.

'So, come here, you big galoot, and give me a hug. I know you didn't mean it.' Nell held her arms out and Pippa hugged her back. 'You were just being you.'

'Well, I'm going to think more about being me and what that is, before I do something like that again. Seriously, Nell, I am so sorry I went for you.'

'I know you are. And I know you didn't mean it. And you know what? I should have told you both at the time. That was the second mistake I made.'

'What was the first?'

'Taking that shortcut along the river. I thought I was invincible. It was a good wakeup call in life.'

'Friends?' Pippa rested her head on Nell's shoulder and her voice was muffled.

'You think you were going to get rid of me that easily? No way, girlfriend. You're stuck with me as a friend until we're old and grey-haired and on our walking frames.'

'Good.' Pippa stepped away and wiped her eyes.

'There's no need to cry.'

'They're happy tears. Come on, we'll go and see what GG's got to offer.' Pippa put one hand on her hip and Nell linked arms with her. 'I don't know how she's going to fit in.'

'It's going to be interesting.' The smile stayed on Nell's face as they walked to the bar. It had been a good night so far.

***

Pippa

The night in the bar was more than interesting. Tam met them halfway along the beach before they got to the bar. The music coming from the sound system was loud.

'Pleased to see you pair haven't killed each other,' she said drily.

'Of course, we haven't. A minor tiff,' Pippa said. 'First one we've had for ages. All good, and all happy here.' Now that she'd apologised to Nell—and Nell was cool with her— she was floating on air again. She reached into her pocket and rubbed her fingers over the ring that Rafe had brought home from England.

'Excellent.' Tam said. 'So, you're in a good mood, boss?'

'Boss? Pippa screwed her face up. 'What's this "boss" shit?'

'I think you're going to need it.'

'Need what?'

'A good mood. I'd hate for you to get stuck into me next.' Tam turned and led the way to the bar. 'It's my fault.'

'What's your fault?'

'You'll see.'

144

The lights of the bar were all on as they stepped from the bush into the cleared area. Strange music was blaring over the sound system. Evie was standing at the bar holding a drink, her eyes wide when she saw the three of them walk in. Nat and Rafe were sitting at a table, each holding a tall coloured cocktail decorated with pineapple leaves.

Pippa looked around. 'Where's Gina?'

'Um, she just went for a break. I suggested it might be an idea if she got some fresh air,' Tam said with a strange look on her face.

'Fresh air?'

Tam nodded. 'I'm sorry, Pip. I think I've stuffed up with this one.'

'Gina? It wasn't just on your recommendation. Her references were excellent.'

'Hmm,' Nell intervened. 'You know how sometimes people give a good reference to get rid of someone they don't want?'

'Okay, what's she done? And can you please turn that music down. Or better still, turn it off.'

As Tam headed to the sound system they'd installed behind the bar, Pippa walked over to the table where Rafe and Nat were sitting looking bemused. As well as the two coloured cocktails, there was a box of cards there. She picked the box up and read the label.

'*Tarot d'Amour?* What are these for?' The label on the box was graphic to say the least. She narrowed her eyes and peered close. The blonde model on the cover of the box was wearing very little and looked very much like GG.

It was GG!

Rafe chuckled. 'Apparently, they're guaranteed to improve anyone's sex life.'

Nat grinned and didn't say anything, and Pippa put the box down when she heard Tam's laughing snort behind her. Before she could turn around, two firm hands grabbed her shoulders as a musky perfume surrounded her.

'Come see, boss *bebe*. I'm goin' to show you how good I am, me.'

Pippa turned around and looked up at GG. Her cheeks were flushed, and her lips were lifted in a crazy grin.

'I beg your pardon?'

'Come with me, *bebe* and I'll mis . . . mix you three ladies, a cocktail to knock your li'l ole socks off. And then we're goin' to play some fun games.'

Evie put a hand over her mouth and giggled, and Tam snorted again as Gina sashayed over to the bar. Pippa followed her.

'You do know tonight was a trial run to see if you were suitable.' Her mouth dropped open when she saw what GG was wearing. The shortest skirt that Pippa had ever seen, and unbelievably, a red suspender belt and black fishnet stockings.

'*Le fe cho,*' Gina said as she picked up a handful of ice, ran it over her flushed cheeks and then dropped it down the front of her lowcut black top with a smile in Rafe's direction.

'What?' Pippa's blood began to boil. She turned around to Evie, Tam and Nell who were all smiling. Rafe quickly dropped the grin when he saw the expression on Pippa's face. 'Is she drunk?' she hissed. 'What is '*le fe cho*? A cocktail?'

Gina rolled her eyes and almost purred. 'No, *bebe*. It means it's hot in here, and I'm hoping it might get a little hotter when we get to the cards.'

Tam snorted again. 'Sorry, Pip,' she muttered.

Pippa narrowed her eyes as Gina tried to reach for a glass and missed it. 'Are you drunk?'

'Oh, maybe just a little one or two while I was waiting for you to come.'

Pippa looked at her. 'I'll have champagne, please.'

'Oh, no *dahlin*. You ain't havin that bubble stuff. Three more cocktails coming up.'

'No. That's enough.' Pippa's voice was like steel. 'Come back to the house with me please, Gina. We are going to have a little chat.'

Chapter Twenty

Nell

By the time Pippa came back to the bar—alone—
they'd cleaned up the bar. Two broken glasses, and a
smear of cream and chopped pineapple over most of the
counter.

Tam's mood moved between giggles and
worrying. 'We've left this too late. There's no way we'll
be able to find someone suitable for the bar before the
big opening next Saturday night.'

Nell nodded. 'After that experience, Pippa will
be way more careful. No more relying on word of mouth
or references. Interviews from now on.'

'Was Gina like that when you worked with her?'

'She was a good worker, but yeah, I suppose she
was a bit out there.' Tam picked up the pineapple pieces
and put them in the bin beneath the bar. 'What a waste.
But she was nowhere near like that. And you know
what?' She tipped her head to the side. I don't ever
remember the Cajun accent or the French words.'

'Just goes to show. Take references with a grain
of salt,' Nell said.

'As long as Pippa's not too upset. We're going to
have to work mighty hard to get someone before next
weekend.'

As always when Nat came anywhere near Nell,
she sensed him before she turned.

'Ah, ladies?' he said with a grin.

'Don't you start on me, Nat. I've got to face the
music when Pippa gets back,' Tam said putting the last
of the mess in the bin.

'Here she is now,' he said catching Nell's eye. A quiver tugged at her lower belly, and she dropped her eyes, pretending to focus on the cleaning cloth.

Nat cleared his throat. 'Nell?'

She looked up and held his gaze. 'Yep. What's up?'

'I've got an idea to run past you. Solves a couple of problems, but I want to run it by you before I talk to Pippa. Come outside with me for a sec?'

Evie had gone to her room, using the excuse of an early night, and Rafe was sitting at the table flicking through Gina's tarot cards. Every so often, he would chuckle and shake his head.

Nell pointed to the door on the beach side and Nat followed her out. They hadn't gone far when he touched her elbow and she looked down at his hand, quite happy for him to touch her.

No tensing and no flight or fight response. She smiled. 'What's up?'

'Well, I want to check with you before I suggest this to Pippa.' Nat's eyes held Nell's and a shimmery feeling ran all the way down to her toes.

'What would that be?' Her tone was maybe a little bit shorter than usual because she was trying to ignore the way her nerves were going haywire.

'I need a place to live for a while, and you gals need someone to man the bar. I've got my bar tickets and a heap of experience in bar work. Do you think it would be over the top to run that by Pippa?'

Nell tapped her top lip with her index finger, thinking what it would mean if Nat was on site.

Only if we had more computer problems, nothing else, she tried to tell myself. If Nat was here, the network would run like clockwork. Someone they knew and they all liked would be in the bar, and they already had a spare room where Nat could bunk down.

Nell growled silently at the little voice in her head to shut up. *And Nat would be here all the time.*

But her mouth ran away with her thoughts before she could put a stop on it. 'And you'd be here to help me desensitise.'

'It sounds like a win-win situation to me,' he said.

Nell nodded and went to the doorway. 'Pip. You got a minute?'

Despite the fiasco with Gina, Pippa was still smiling; Nell had never seen her look so happy. If she was a person who believed in auras, she would have said Pippa's was shining tonight.

'How did that go?' Nell asked hesitantly.

'What? With GG?' Pippa shook her head and chuckled. 'We've come to a mutual agreement and I've already called Jiminy He'll be here at 7.30 in the morning. She said she didn't like the bar and wasn't happy about staying so I didn't have to sack her before she even started.'

'Phew. Pip? Nat's got an idea.'

She tipped her head to the side and levelled her intense gaze at him. Pip could be scary at times, but the soft smile on her lips dispelled that tonight. 'Yep?'

'Fire away, Nat,' Nell said.

Once Nat had outlined what he'd suggested to her, Pippa smiled. 'That's a fantastic idea. Are you sure it won't take away from your work?'

Nat's smile was wide. 'You would be doing me a huge favour. Only thing I'd have to ask for is a room with a bit of space to put a couple of computers. Even down the back of one the garden sheds would do. I had a bit of a look at them before. There's power down there.'

'If there's one thing, we've got plenty of,' Pippa said. 'It's room. It sounds like a great solution to me. What do you think, Nell?' Her glance was wary.

'Perfect,' Nell said.

Pippa held out her hand and shook Nat's firmly 'We have a deal. Only one thing I want to ask you.'

Nat shot a worried glance at Nell. 'Yes?'

'Could you start now? Rafe and I have some news to tell you all.'

Chapter Twenty-One

Nell

That night in the bar celebrating Rafe and Pippa's engagement was one of the happiest nights of Nell's life. Rafe had stood and told them that Pippa had accepted his proposal. And Tam and Nell had swooped on her screaming with happiness.

'Gina's snoring in the back room,' Evie told us with a grin.

'As long as she doesn't miss her boat tomorrow,' Pippa added. 'I'm afraid I don't want to see her again.'

Nat was kept busy behind the bar and there were a few empty bottles of bubbles by the end of the night. Rafe had insisted on top shelf, and said he would pick up the tab.

'It's not every night a man gets engaged,' he said with his arms around Pippa.

As for Pippa, she was absolutely glowing.

Nell kept looking at her and was ashamed to admit that her friend's happiness made her the tiniest bit jealous.

She shook herself. No, Pippa deserved every minute of it. 'So, when's the wedding?' she asked with a smile. 'I know this really good island to come to for your honeymoon'.

'Ha ha,' Pippa said 'And don't worry, it won't be for a while. But one thing, if it's okay with you girls.' She looked from Tam to Nell to Evie. 'I'm going to move up to Rafe's house.'

'Of course, it's okay,' they all rushed to say.

'It leaves a big room for Nat to move into, with all his computers. I'll take you over to the mainland in a day or so, Nat, and you can get what you need.'

'Thank you, Pippa', Nat said.

Eventually the party broke up, and Rafe and Pippa headed back up the hill. Evie went to bed with a yawn, and Tam carried the leftovers back to the kitchen in the house.

Nell sat at the bar while Nat rinsed the glasses and wiped down the countertop. When he'd finished, he came around the bar and sat beside her.

'How about a night cap?'

'I think that's a good idea. I'm too pumped to get to sleep. What a day it's been.' Despite her words, a yawn blurred them.

'What would you like?' Nat asked.

Nell was aware of him looking at her and looked down at her hands, ignoring that warm rush that she'd had on and off all day. 'Would I sound silly if I just asked for some warm milk in the microwave? That'll help me sleep.'

'Whatever works.'

Five minutes later, she'd finished her warm milk, and Nat switched the light off in the bar.

They walked along the path, close to each other but not touching, with an awkward silence between them.

We had almost reached the house when Nell stopped. 'Nat?'

'What's wrong?'

'Nothing. I just wanted . . . I just wanted to ask you something. Two things actually.'

His eyes shone in the moonlight, but his brow was wrinkled. 'Yes?'

'Would you, would you hold my hand again? Just practice, you know.'

He reached for her hand and as his fingers curled around hers the strangest feeling of all being right with the world overcame Nell.

'What was the second thing?' he asked softly.

'Um. Now that you're going to be here for a while would you make up a schedule?'

'A schedule for what?'

'For me. For that desensitisation stuff.' She knew she was speaking too quickly but was embarrassed to ask. 'I'll leave it to you. You know. First week, hold my hand, second week, maybe try to put your arm around me to see how I cope. You know stuff like that.'

It sounded so stupid when she put it into words, but Nat nodded, and his expression was serious.

'I'm sure I could manage that. Do you want me to send you those articles I read?'

Nell shook her head. 'No. I'll leave it all in your hands.'

'Okay. I'll work something out. Do we need a contract or anything?'

'Oh, heck no. It'll just be something on the side while you're here working the bar and looking after the network. And um, living here until your house is fixed.'

'Good, not a problem,' he said briskly. His words were what she wanted to hear, but Nat had a strange distant look in his eyes, and for a minute Nell thought she'd said the wrong thing. But her hand stayed in his as they walked towards the house, and into the office.

'Are you happy to sleep on the sofa bed in here tonight until we get organised?'

'That's fine. Anyway, I'm tired. I'll see you tomorrow.'

She looked at Nat, and for a moment was tempted to stand on her toes and brush a kiss across his cheek, but common sense chimed in.

Nell knew she was a job to him, and the last thing he would want was an old friend mooning over him.

'You know where the bathroom and everything is? I'll put a towel out for you.'

'Thank you.'

The silence was long, and she shuffled backwards towards the door. 'Okay, night, Nat. And thank you for everything.'

'Good night, Nell. I'll see you in the morning.'

***

Nat Dwyer lay on the sofa bed for a long time before sleep claimed him.

Was agreeing to help Nell a good move or not?

He was damned if he did and damned if he didn't. All he'd wanted to do was take her in his arms tonight and hold her and keep her safe from her fears.

Over ten years ago, he'd fallen for this gentle woman, and it had broken his heart when she had wiped him. He'd got over his broken heart that day in the office where she'd worked, where she had spoken to him so rudely.

Now he knew why she had done that, it made it a little easier to bear, but it had brought all of his feelings for her screaming back. Nat knew he had no chance with

Nell. She'd always thought of him as a womaniser, and she had no reason to change her mind. He was big enough to help her through this and help let her learn to trust again.

Could he go softly, softly, and show her that he wasn't that man she'd thought he was?

Nat rolled over and punched his pillow.

Maybe if he gave it his best shot.

And he was going to.

Chapter Twenty-Two

Nell

The week before the bar opening flew by. Tam was cranky as she immersed herself in menus and orders, and Nell soon learned to keep out of her way. Evie was out in the garden from daylight until dark, mowing, and putting the finishing touches on the gardens around the huts.

Pippa seemed to be everywhere, supervising, barking orders, and worrying about what could go wrong.

But she always had a smile on her face.

Nat was busy setting up his own network; Pippa had taken him over to the mainland and he'd brought most of his gear back. Since then he'd spent a lot of time in the front room, setting it up.

When he wasn't there, he was down in the bar, reorganising it to suit him.

'What's got you looking so unhappy?' Pippa pulled Nell up two days before the opening. She was sitting on the front veranda looking across the water. The smell of freshly mown grass drifted across from the side of the house, and the smell of something delectable baking came from the kitchen.

Nell lifted her head. 'Me? I'm okay.'

'No, you're not, Nell. I know you too well. Spit it out. What's on your mind? Is it Nat? You two have been mooning about looking at each other all week. Every time he looks the other way, you're looking at him, and he's the same with you.'

'No. No way.' Nell frowned.

Pippa huffed. 'Trust me, Nellie. He's got it bad for you, and at a guess, I'd say you wouldn't be unhappy about that. Tam agrees with me.'

'Don't be silly. I'm just bored. You need to find me a job to do. Since Nat's got the network running smoothly, everything is up to date, and it only takes me a couple of hours in the morning to get the accounts done and check the online bookings.'

'Okay. I've got a job for you.'

Nell glanced across at Pippa, because there was something in her tone, but her expression was innocent.

'What sort of job?'

'I think you need to go down and help Nat in the bar. He's going to be run off his feet on Saturday night. I've had so many more people say they're coming over; the bay's going to be full of boats.'

'You mean get ready for the night, or help him in there?'

'Both. You can clear glasses and that sort of thing, can't you?'

'I guess so.'

'Go down to the bar now. Nat's down there. I was just talking to him. He seemed a bit stressed.' Pippa looked at her from beneath her lashes.

'What about?'

Pippa shrugged. 'I don't know. You're mates with him. Maybe you could ask if everything's okay? We can't afford to lose him now. We'd really be up shit creek if we did. Can I leave it to you to sort out?'

'Okay. I'll go down there now.'

Nell didn't see Pippa's devious smile as she headed into her room to comb her hair and put some lip gloss on.

A groan escaped Nell's lips as she walked towards the bar. Nat was stocking the two big fridges at the back with beer. Jiminy had delivered another load of food and drink this morning.

The weather was warming up quickly and Nat had taken his shirt off. She watched the play of muscles across his tanned back as he lifted each carton across from the counter to the fridge. A warm feeling gripped her lower belly, and a shiver ran down her back, and it had nothing to do with being scared. Her lips parted and she took her pleasure watching him.

She stood there for a full five minutes and jumped when Nat called over his shoulder. 'Are you going to just stand there gawking, or are you going to give me a hand?'

'Sorry. I was daydreaming.'

The look he gave her was interesting.

Nell hurried over. 'How can I help?'

'If you hold the door open for me, it would make a difference. Just until I get these bigger cartons to the top shelf.' Nell did as he asked, and he'd soon loaded the shelves.

'I've just got to get rid of these boxes and I'm done. If you want to go. Thanks for your help.'

Nell shook her head. 'No. I'll keep you company for a while. I was . . . I was . . . um. . . wondering if you'd thought any more about my program.'

'Which program? The accounting package, you mean.' Nat lifted his arm and wiped the perspiration from his brow with his forearm and Nell's breath caught in her throat, as the combined smell of sweat and man hit her.

'Um, no. My program. You know, touching me and everything.' Her face heated as she realised what she'd said.

Touching me!

Nat took a step closer to her and his eyes narrowed. 'I have. Do you want to practise now? Maybe I should surprise you, so you don't know what's coming and see how you handle that.' His eyes were dark and intent on hers. 'What would you think about that? DO you think you could cope with some surprises?'

Nell lifted her chin. 'I think I could cope.'

Nat came closer and she leaned back against the wall, not knowing what to expect. What was his second move going to be? Touch her elbow? Put his arms around her.

Oh, she wished, how she wished.

Nell looked up and he held her gaze as he lifted one arm above her shoulder, and then put his hand on the wall to her left. Slowly he lifted his other arm, and she waited for his touch, but he put it on the wall on the other side of her head, effectively trapping her.

'Are you okay?' His face was only a few centimetres from hers, and her breathing quickened.

She nodded mutely.

'You seem to have been going okay this week, so I thought I might skip a few steps. Sort of like shock therapy.'

Nell held his eyes and nodded. Nat was so close to her now his breath was warming her lips. She didn't move a muscle as his head lowered and his lips slid over hers. Shock, but no fear rocketed through her. She didn't move as his lips played over hers. Eventually, she lifted her hand and placed it against his bare chest, but his lips stayed where they were.

'Are you coping?' he murmured against her mouth.

'I am. Very well,' she replied, surprised by the desperate need that was rising in her. The need for him to stay there. A need she had never felt before. Nell squeezed her eyes shut, willing him to stay.

'Still okay?' His mouth was firm on hers now, almost demanding, and Nell opened her lips to give him access. Her legs were shaking so much, she could barely stand, and she grabbed onto his waist with her other hand. His bare skin was sleek and smooth beneath her touch and she was gratified by his small intake of breath.

Maybe it was more than helping her for Nat?

Maybe she could dream?

For the first time in a long time, Nell stopped thinking things through and surrendered to her feelings.

Need pulsed through her in time with the beat of her heart. Like a flower unfurling its petals to the warm sun, Nell felt herself opening to him. No fear, no worry and no self-consciousness.

Nat moved away and loss hit her like a physical jolt. Reaching out again, she opened her eyes. His were guarded as he looked at her. Leaving her hand on his chest, she looked him square in the face.

'Thank you.'

'For?' His voice shook a little and hope unfurled in her chest.

'For showing me how I feel.'

'How do you feel?' Nat lowered his arms and put his hands on her shoulders. His touch was gentle, and she kept her eyes on his face as she leaned into him. A slow smile lifted his lips.

'I feel . . . I feel happy that I *know* how I feel now. I'm happy that I can admit it. And not be embarrassed, and not be scared.'

His voice was low, and his lips hovered over hers. 'Tell me, Nell. What were you scared of?'

'I was scared that I wanted you, and you didn't want me.'

The groan that came from Nat as he wrapped his arms around her told her everything she wanted to know.

'Pippa came to see me,' he said. 'She gave me some hope. That's why I tried the shock therapy.'

'I like the shock therapy.' Nell knew her smile was shy. 'It worked.'

Nat's head lowered to hers, and Nell put her arms around him. Her fingers played over his skin; she couldn't stop touching him.

'I'm very happy it did. Do you know how long I've been waiting to kiss you?' he asked.

'How long?' she whispered against his mouth.

'About eleven years. We've got a lot of catching up to do.'

Nat's head lowered to hers as he proceeded to catch up, that until a voice interrupted them.

'About time,' Pippa said, but she was smiling. 'Sorry to disturb you guys, but we came down for a drink. We have some new arrivals.'

Nell lifted her head and peered around Nat's shoulder and let out a squeal. Eliza and Phillipe were standing next to Pippa.

She looked back to Nat shyly, still not able to believe that he had kissed her. That he cared about her. And being in his arms had felt right.

Perfect.

'It looks like we're all here for the opening. Come and meet Eliza and Phillipe,' she said, but her smile was for Nat.

He threaded his fingers through hers and held Nell close as they walked across to the others.

'Looks like you've been busy while we've been gone,' Eliza said.

Nell nodded. 'We all have.'

Nat slipped his shirt on as the introductions were made. In her fluster, Nell hadn't noticed the other woman who was standing near Eliza.

'Nell, this is my friend, Sienna. She's come to stay for a while,' Eliza said. 'And we've got news. Fabulous news that's going to make a huge difference to Ma Carmichael's.'

Phillipe nodded. 'It is the best news we could bring back with us.'

'Don't keep us in suspense.' Pippa was almost jumping out of her skin. 'Spill. What news?'

Eliza shook her head. 'Wait until Tam and Evie join us. And Rafe. It's time for a big celebration.'

THE END

What news have Eliza and Phillipe brought home from Europe? And why is Tamsin upset with the changes that it will make to Ma Carmichael's?

Tamsin Jones has invested a lot of time and energy in the restaurant at the new eco-resort developed by her friend, Pippa, on Pentecost Island. The dynamics of the work team—and their lifelong friendship— changed with the return of Eliza Pengelly, and the mysterious sailor, Phillipe.

The restaurant is about to open when the arrival of another stranger on the island seems to put the project at risk. Tamsin is determined to discover what secret the sexy Gabe Kent is hiding—and why he is so interested in her . . . and the island.

Gabe has a promise to fulfil, but Tamsin seems to be shadowing him, the closer he gets to completing the task he has been entrusted with. It should be easy to ignore her and complete his task. . . but Gabe has never been so attracted to a woman before.

Can he redeem himself and save his heart in the process?

Island Charm is available in eBook and print

OTHER BOOKS from ANNIE

Whitsunday Dawn
Undara
Osprey Reef
East of Alice
Porter Sisters Series
Kakadu Sunset
Daintree
Diamond Sky
Hidden Valley
Larapinta
Kakadu Dawn
Pentecost Island Series
Pippa
Eliza
Nell
Tamsin
Evie
Cherry
Odessa
Sienna
Tess
Isla
The Augathella Girls Series
Outback Roads
Outback Sky
Outback Escape
Outback Wind
Outback Dawn
Outback Moonlight
Outback Dust
Outback Hope

Sunshine Coast Series
Waiting for Ana
The Trouble with Jack
Healing His Heart
Sunshine Coast Boxed Set

The Richards Brothers Series
The Trouble with Paradise
Marry in Haste
Outback Sunrise
Richards Brothers Boxed Set

Bondi Beach Love Series
Beach House
Beach Music
Beach Walk
Beach Dreams
The House on the Hill

Second Chance Bay Series
Her Outback Playboy
Her Outback Protector
Her Outback Haven
Her Outback Paradise
The McDougalls of Second Chance Bay Boxed Set

Love Across Time Series
Come Back to Me
Follow Me
Finding Home
The Threads that Bind

Bindarra Creek
Worth the Wait
Full Circle
Secrets of River Cottage

Four Seasons Short and Sweet
Ten Days in Paradise
Follow the Sun
Others
Deadly Secrets
Adventures in Time
Silver Valley Witch
The Emerald Necklace
Christmas with the Boss
Her Christmas Star
An Aussie Christmas Duo (two Christmas novellas)
A Clever Christmas

About the Author

Author of the Year Ausrom Readers' Choice 2014
Best Established Author Ausrom Readers' Choice 2015
Finalist for Author of the Year, Book of the Year, Cover of the Year, Ausrom Readers' Choice 2016
Best Established Author, Ausrom Readers' Choice 2017
Book of the Year (Whitsunday Dawn) Ausrom Readers' Choice Awards 2018

Annie lives in Australia, on the beautiful north coast of New South Wales. She sits in her writing chair and looks out over the tranquil Pacific Ocean. She has fulfilled her lifelong dream of becoming an author and is producing books at a prolific rate.

She writes contemporary romance and loves telling the stories that always have a happily ever after. She lives with her very own hero of many years and they share their home with Toby, the naughtiest dog in the universe, and Barney, the rag doll kitten, who hides when the grandchildren come to visit.

Stay up to date with her latest releases at her website: http://www.annieseaton.net

If you would like to stay up to date with Annie's releases, subscribe to her newsletter on her website.

www.ingramcontent.com/pod-product-compliance
Lightning Source LLC
Chambersburg PA
CBHW030431120726
47903CB00003B/916